"Why are you bothering with me?" Caitlin asked furiously. **"I mean, if you think I'm skinny and stressed-out and—"**

"I never said you were skinny," Mike replied defensively. "I said you're very tense and you probably don't eat right. But for the record, I think you're gorgeous, and I'd be more comfortable if you weren't so—so womanly.

"Did you hear me, Miss Grant? I said you're gorgeous and I meant it. And you'd still be gorgeous if you fleshed out those fantastic bones of yours a little. And the reason I'm wasting time with you . . . well, it's beyond me. Because you're trouble, Caitlin Grant, the kind of trouble I've avoided for a long time. If I had any sense, I'd stay away from you. But there's one problem. . . ." His self-control vanished. "This problem," he said, hauling her into his arms and taking the kiss he'd been craving since the moment they met.

Caitlin's shocked gasp was lost in the mouth that pressed against hers. Too sudden, she thought dizzily. Too fast. Too unexpected. And too delicious to resist. . . .

WHAT ARE *LOVESWEPT* ROMANCES?

They are stories of true romance and touching emotion. We believe those two very important ingredients are constants in our highly sensual and very believable stories in the *LOVESWEPT* line. Our goal is to give you, the reader, stories of consistently high quality that may sometimes make you laugh, sometimes make you cry, but are always fresh and creative and contain many delightful surprises within their pages.

Most romance fans read an enormous number of books. Those they truly love, they keep. Others may be traded with friends and soon forgotten. We hope that each *LOVESWEPT* romance will be a treasure—a "keeper." We will always try to publish

LOVE STORIES YOU'LL NEVER FORGET
BY AUTHORS YOU'LL ALWAYS REMEMBER

The Editors

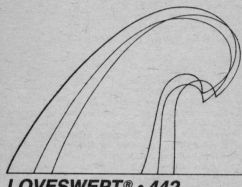

LOVESWEPT® • 442

Gail Douglas
It Had to Be You

BANTAM BOOKS
NEW YORK • TORONTO • LONDON • SYDNEY • AUCKLAND

TO EILEEN

For after-school cocoa, long letters from Cedar Lake, clothes tips, dating advice, a shoulder to cry on, corny jokes, pep talks, baby-sitting, inspiration, nudges in the right direction, and occasional kick-starts ... thanks.

IT HAD TO BE YOU

A Bantam Book / December 1990

If you would be interested in receiving protective vinyl covers for your Loveswept books, please write to this address for information:

Loveswept
Bantam Books
P. O. Box 985
Hicksville, NY 11802

ISBN 0-553-44073-X

Published simultaneously in the United States and Canada

Bantam Books are published by Bantam Books, a division of Bantam Doubleday Dell Publishing Group, Inc. Its trademark, consisting of the words "Bantam Books" and the portrayal of a rooster, is Registered in U.S. Patent and Trademark Office and in other countries. Marca Registrada. Bantam Books, 666 Fifth Avenue, New York, New York 10103.

PRINTED IN THE UNITED STATES OF AMERICA

OPM   0 9 8 7 6 5 4 3 2 1

One

Mike Harris could have sworn that the deck of the *Queen Elizabeth 2* had shifted under his feet.

Interesting, he thought as his pulse bolted like a startled racehorse. He hadn't boarded the ship yet.

All he'd done was indulge in a quick once-over of a tall brunette in the lineup to his left, and suddenly the pier had rocked like a balsa raft caught by a high wave.

He looked at his wristwatch, studying it intently though he knew the time, anything to keep from staring at the legs . . . the woman . . . beside him.

Mike couldn't figure his reaction. Granted, the lady had brightened the scene on the crowded pier in her formfitting yellow minidress, bounding toward the row of check-in counters like an exuberant gazelle, her slender body and endless legs making his most basic male instincts lurch to attention. But for the earth to move? Ridiculous.

He decided to venture a second glance, betting himself that the lady wasn't all that gorgeous. Second glances at attractive ladies almost always brought disappointment.

But he found himself tumbling into an iridescent abyss as almond-shaped sea-green eyes gazed directly back at him, sparkling with excitement and impish humor and an innocent sensuality that was underscored by full, slightly parted coral-tinted lips.

So much for disappointment, Mike thought as the floor teetered again and his pulse broke into a full-fledged gallop. "Hi," he heard himself say in a strangled voice. He had no idea why he'd spoken.

Caitlin Grant started, realizing that the tall, dark, handsome stranger straight out of a Gypsy fortune teller's crystal ball had caught her gaping at him. Sudden warmth suffused her face and throat. "Hi," she said with a tiny smile, searching her mind for some witty follow-up. When she came up empty, she simply lowered her gaze and stared at her feet as if she'd never noticed them before.

Wondering why the woman's monosyllable had affected him like a siren song, Mike tightened his grip on the handle of his briefcase and let his gaze move slowly over her. He took in the elfin cut of her chestnut hair, the graceful column of her neck, the curves of her trim figure, the sleek golden legs, and the prettiest feet he'd ever seen, utterly feminine in delicate, low-heeled yellow sandals, which showed off toenails tipped a soft coral shade.

He took a deep, steadying breath and searched for some negative quality to temper the perfect picture and restore some of his usual detachment. The only flaw he could come up with—and it wasn't much, but he was desperate—was a certain confusion in the woman's image: Her short hair and zippy little dress were as up-to-date as next month's *Vogue* cover, but her manner was straight out of the nineteenth century, complete with demurely lowered lashes. She'd even blushed. How long had it been since he'd seen a woman blush?

He took another controlled breath and let it out on a count of eight, refusing to be charmed by natural pink highlights on elegant cheekbones. Blushing, fragile young things weren't for him. Now, if only his heartbeat would get the message and slow down a little . . .

"Miss?" the check-in agent said as he sent the couple in front of the woman on their way, embarkation passes in hand.

Lost in her private thoughts, she didn't look up.

"Excuse me, miss," the agent said in a polite but weary English accent. "Your ticket, please?"

When she still didn't respond, Mike shocked himself by reaching out to touch her arm, his fingers feather-light against her warm, soft skin.

She jumped as if someone had dropped an ice cube down the back of her dress. "What?" she cried, her eyes huge.

She was like a skittish colt, Mike thought, pulling back his hand almost guiltily. "Your ticket," he said calmly. "The agent is ready for you."

Caitlin's skin was consumed by hot flames as she heard a man chuckling in the lineup behind her. "Thank you," she said, favoring Mike with another nervous little smile. "I guess I was . . . daydreaming." She didn't consider it necessary to explain what she'd been daydreaming about. The stupid blush was saying it all. Twenty-eight years old and discovering for the first time what it felt like to turn scarlet. Wonderful, she thought.

Stepping up to the counter, she slid the narrow strap of her white leather handbag off her shoulder and began fumbling with the clasp. "Sorry," she murmured to the agent as he waited patiently for her to produce her ticket. "New purse. You know how stubborn these snaps can be. . . ."

"Oh, of course," the man drawled, resting his chin on his hand. "My own little beaded number gives me the same problem."

Caitlin looked up just in time to catch the large, square-jawed agent—about as effeminate as John Wayne—exchanging a man-to-man grin with the handsome stranger who'd caused all the trouble in the first place.

With a scowl Caitlin tugged hard on the clasp. It finally let go, but the sudden jerk made the contents of the bag spew out and clatter to the floor—lipstick, compact, pens, notebooks, passport, and ticket.

Mike immediately put down his briefcase and bent to retrieve the scattered items.

Unfortunately, Caitlin dived at the same instant to scoop up what she could. Crashing into what felt like a chunk of granite but turned out to be a broad male shoulder, she lost her balance and landed on her bottom, her dress riding dangerously high on her thighs while she braced herself with her palms on the floor behind her, barely managing to stay in a semirespectable sitting position.

Mike swallowed hard as he stared at her. Not your type, Harris, he reminded himself with near-desperation.

The luminous green eyes seemed about to spill over as another burst of laughter from the lineup suggested that some creep was getting a kick out of the lady's embarrassment. Mike felt a sudden tightness in his chest, a strange kind of squeezing sensation. "Sorry," he said, his voice breaking like a teenager's. He cleared his throat. "Sorry," he said again, an octave lower. As one more male chortle sounded, he narrowed his eyes and sent a sweeping glance over the line until it landed on the source of the misplaced glee, a plaid-jacketed man whose grin faded under Mike's quelling glare.

Mike did a rapid visual survey of the damage, spied the lady's passport and ticket, and grabbed them as he straightened up, at the same time extending a hand to help her to her feet.

Caitlin hesitated, suspecting she would live to regret touching this particular man even innocently. Seeing few options short of being rude, however, she accepted the hand he offered and concentrated on blocking the heat that instantly radiated into her from the point of contact.

"Forgive me," Mike said, putting her passport and ticket on the counter as he drew her to a standing position. He wasn't sure why he was apologizing, or why this particular female seemed to have brought out his latent protective instincts; he had to fight an urge to draw her into his arms, to stroke her hair and cuddle her and make her laugh about the whole farce. "I was trying to help, and I made things worse," he said as she reached eye level with him.

Caitlin couldn't summon a word. She just stared. What a wonderful face, she thought, her silly humiliation receding as the entire scene faded into a fuzzy background, leaving only chiseled features to be imprinted on her consciousness, along with expressive dark eyes and blue-black hair and a tempting mouth. "My fault," she said after a very long moment. "And you did help. Thanks."

Mike began to wonder if the crew of the ocean liner would toss a life preserver to a passenger who was managing to drown without leaving the pier. Struggling against the pull of a powerful undertow, he gave the lady a strained grin. "Let's try the drill again; I'll pick up your things while you get checked in, all right?"

Caitlin nodded, though she was vaguely surprised at herself for entrusting her purse and its contents to a complete stranger. Not that he was likely to snatch it; her practiced eye had already judged his taupe linen suit to be an Armani, his briefcase and loafers to be from Gucci, his aftershave to be subtle and expensive.

As he crouched down to gather her belongings, Caitlin tried in vain to drag her gaze from him. She couldn't understand why the man's impact on her was so potent. As a rule she wasn't attracted to his type—obviously successful. She admired society's rebels, not its establishment icons. And a male like this one, who projected the tense aura of a cougar about to pounce, was her idea of bad news even if he did have eyes like a sunlit mountain lake. Besides, he was too young, too coiled for action, to appeal to her. She preferred older men who were undemanding and easygoing.

"Miss Grant?" she heard her agent say, though his voice seemed to be coming from a distance. "Is Miss Caitlin Grant still in the vicinity?"

She gave a small start, then turned and laughed, her inherent good humor returning as she watched her embarkation card being prepared. "I guess I'm just excited about this trip," she said, finally managing to come up with an excuse for her addled behavior. "It's something I've dreamed of since I was a little girl."

"And may your voyage with us be most memorable," the agent said in his plummy accent. "It certainly should be; you've been upgraded, Miss Grant."

Caitlin tilted her head to one side and gave him

a puzzled look as he ticked off her new cabin number, explaining that she'd been moved from Three Deck to One Deck. "But I was already booked into first class," she protested mildly, though she knew it was subdivided into various categories. "Why would I be upgraded? Are you sure?"

"Very sure, but I'm afraid I've no idea why." The agent grinned. "Never look a gift sea horse in the mouth, Miss Grant. Neptune is smiling on you. Accept and enjoy." As he continued filling out cards and forms and checking her passport and whatever else he had to do, Caitlin's attention was recaptured by the man behind her, who was drawing himself up to his full height and handing over her purse, looking more alarmed than predatory.

Mike's mouth had gone dry, and his pulse had careened right out off the track. He'd been telling himself she was probably booked into second class and would disappear the minute she boarded the ship. Out of sight and, with any luck, soon out of mind. Not only had he been dead wrong, but he'd just learned that her cabin was unnervingly close to his.

He struggled in vain to resist the pull of her bottomless green eyes, beginning to worry. Was this lady short-circuiting the wiring of his defense system?

"Again, thank you," Caitlin said with a catch in her voice. The air seemed to crackle with electricity, powerful currents forming a magnetic connection between herself and this total stranger. She had to put in a breaker, she told herself. Immediately. Looping the purse strap over her shoulder, she forced herself to turn back to the Cunard agent. He was holding out her embarkation card and other documentation. "Thank you too," she said brightly. "I'm sure I'll have an absolutely wonderful voyage." And she *was* sure about the voyage. It *was* a dream come true.

She had somewhat less confidence about what she was going to do at the end of the transatlantic crossing. She was overly sensitive and nervous about her plans to set off alone on a walking tour of the Cotswolds in England. In the past she'd always had some friend along for company, but her former companions had settled into marriage or careers and couldn't join her this time.

She listened absently to the ticket agent's rapid-fire instructions for getting to her cabin, but she wasn't hearing him very well; the doubts that were plaguing her had come back in a rush.

During the weeks leading up to her departure date, she'd begun to question her way of life, to wonder if she was forever uprooting herself out of habit rather than real desire. Yet she'd barreled ahead, resigning the job that had started to show promise, giving up the apartment that had begun to feel like home, walking away from friends and the little niche she'd carved out in the community.

According to the theory formulated by her best friend, Pam Jennings, Caitlin thought fondly, her wandering existence was a search. But for what? "You're still trying to discover your identity, luv," Pam had said after her initial excitement at Caitlin's phone call had died down, and after she'd offered to share her London flat. "When you lost your parents at the impressionable age of thirteen, you were bound to feel you'd lost yourself as well. Still, pet, you've got to realize you won't find Caitlin Grant by tearing around the world; she's not out there, any more than your mum and dad are. It's all somewhere deep inside you. That's where you have to look."

Caitlin had laughed. "Hey, I just want to explore the country where my father was brought up, Pam. No Freudian undertones. And I've been looking forward to seeing you again, though heaven knows why." Pam had been her roommate at UCLA.

"I want to see you too," Pam had said, relenting for just a moment before taking up her cause again. "But I think what you're really hoping is that you'll bump into the ghosts of John and Maureen Grant, as if they'd left their spiritual imprint on the places where they were so happy."

One thing about Pam, Caitlin thought. She had an unnerving habit of zeroing in on the truth.

Caitlin snapped back to the present as she realized that the agent was giving her another of his quizzical looks.

"Any questions, Miss Grant?"

With one more smile and a shake of her head, Caitlin walked to the gangplank, her heart thudding—in anticipation of the voyage, she told herself.

Determined not to think about mystery men, she focused on the unexpected bonus of an upgrade, a great beginning she was eager to write about in the journal she'd promised to keep for her aunt Penny, who'd made the *QE2* passage possible. Caitlin also realized that going top class would make for extra zip in the columns she'd agreed to send to the little weekly newspaper in St. Petersburg, Florida, where she'd worked.

As she approached the boarding area, Caitlin still wasn't convinced of her good fortune. She half-expected someone to call her back and say there had been a mistake. When no one did, she allowed herself a rush of elation, feeling like a jewel thief who'd unexpectedly got her hands on the Hope diamond.

Waywardly, her thoughts flew to her gorgeous, helpful stranger, but she quickly tamped them down. The man was becoming a nuisance. She had to put him in perspective, though perhaps she would mention him in the journal. Aunt Penny would get a kick out of a hint of romance in the adventure she'd insisted she was going to enjoy vicariously.

Placing her right foot on the gangplank, Caitlin took a deep breath and hesitated for a moment, impressing upon herself that at this very second she was beginning the vacation of a lifetime—two lifetimes: hers and her aunt's. Aunt Penny's adventures had filled many journals, yet the one experience she'd wanted but had never managed was a trip aboard a luxury liner. Thanks to her debilitating arthritis, she never would. Caitlin intended to make every detail of the voyage come alive in her journal.

Allowing herself one casual backward glance, she felt a jolt of excitement go through her. Had the man's dark eyes been on her until she'd turned, or was her imagination playing games?

Games, she decided. With a silent good-bye to Tall, Dark, and Handsome, and to what she assumed was the briefest and most one-sided flirtation in marine history, she gave herself a firm reminder that even if the man was legally, socially, and emotionally available, and even if there was the faintest likelihood that he might be attracted to her, she was *not* interested in that kind of distraction.

Not at all interested, she repeated silently, tingling spine and quickened pulse notwithstanding.

Mike shifted from one foot to the other, annoyed with himself for his sudden impatience.

He had no desire to catch up with Caitlin Grant, so what did it matter that the man behind his particular counter seemed to be a charter member of Slow Agents of America?

But finally he was striding toward the gangplank, managing to beat a couple from another line, keeping them from stepping between him and his lovely quarry.

He couldn't imagine what had got into him.

He was a few feet behind her as they boarded the ship and stood at the entrance of a large circular room, its blue carpeting set off by a gleaming white grand piano in the sunken center area.

Although he had no previous experience with ocean liners, Mike approved of what he saw, deciding that so far the *QE2* was living up to its top-of-the-line billing. More than living up to it, he decided as his glance wandered off for another lingering scan of Caitlin Grant's luxurious legs. They *were* spectacular: long, bare, and tanned; calves curved to perfection; smooth thighs; skin like mocha silk. Delicious. Mike felt another knot of excitement forming in his stomach. The thought of brushing his lips over that enticing skin, of tasting it . . .

Get a grip, he told himself. It was one thing to admire the woman, even to have given her a bit of help when she'd needed it, but he had to keep his libido in check. He wasn't about to suspend his rules just because he was going beyond the three-mile limit.

A young Englishwoman wearing a Cunard badge was checking embarkation cards and giving directions just inside the midship's lobby. "Your cabin is on the next deck up, miss," she said to Caitlin with a pleasant smile. "Take the exit to the left, then use D stairway." Her expression brightened and an interested gleam filled her eyes as she looked past Caitlin to the next person in line.

Caitlin didn't have to turn to know the inspiration for that gleam. She could feel the man's presence just behind her. She was shocked by the flash of intense possessiveness she felt and almost heard herself say, *Back off, lady. I saw him first.*

She had to settle down, Caitlin realized. She would have enough on her mind simply finding her cabin, without looking for man trouble. Let the crew have first dibs. They were better equipped to handle ships that passed in the night. And anyway, it was the worst kind of mistake to be attracted to a male who needed to be caged to keep a horde of other women away from him.

Caitlin scowled. What were those directions again? D stairway, the exit to the left?

She passed through the wide doorway and saw corridors lined with staterooms, so she knew she was doing something right. But did it matter whether she went right or left to find D stairway?

As Mike made his escape from the effusive Cunard woman who'd seemed intent on doing everything to help him get settled but tuck him in, he managed to catch up with Caitlin Grant again. Her stance told him she was slightly lost, and he automatically leapt to her aid, ripples of excitement moving through him despite his private vow to stay away. "To your left, Miss Grant," he said quietly.

The deep, purring sound was close enough to Caitlin's ear to make her jump, and the warm breath that brushed her skin sent frissons of forbidden delight shimmering through her. She recognized the voice. The crisp, clean, heady fragrance. The allure of danger.

She forced herself to look back with a smile. "Thanks. I was about to go to the right, but I always was an up-the-down-staircase sort of person. I drove my high school vice principal crazy."

Mike wondered how Caitlin Grant managed to muddle through life, much less to travel alone. Obviously, she was none too competent when it came to the basics of getting along. A dreamer. A dizzy broad, his plain-speaking buddy Dave would say affectionately. Dave liked dizzy broads. Mike didn't. Fortunately, Caitlin Grant's quirks weren't his problem. He wasn't likely to have much to do with her even if they were neighbors for the next few days, except perhaps to enjoy looking at her from a safe distance. He would be crazy to resist that pleasure. She was exquisite. Perfect in every detail. He even liked her eyebrows—naturally curved, neither bushy nor plucked to a thin line. And the thick dark lashes that fringed her eyes . . . her sea-green eyes . . . her almond-shaped sea-green eyes . . .

Another tightening inside Mike set off a cacophony of warning bells. Those eyes could be fatal to a man's common sense. They could stir his emotions, make him forget everything that was important to him—including a schedule that didn't leave time for getting seriously tangled up with a dizzy broad or any other kind of woman. The bright, self-sufficient ladies he spent time with in New York had agendas of their own; he stayed away from anyone who might pencil him in for a lengthy and complicated commitment.

So why couldn't he stop gazing at this woman?

Caitlin was trying to tear herself loose from the intent dark eyes that held hers. She was beginning to feel like a mesmerized rabbit caught between a leopard's paws, heart pounding, tiny shivers racing through her body, alarm dominated by fascination.

Nonsense, she told herself abruptly. There were no leopards aboard the *QE2*. Everyone knew cats hated water. "You've sailed on this ship before?" she asked, impressing herself both with the calm sound of her voice and the way she started moving, walking with remarkable steadiness.

Mike smiled, amused and amazed by her confusion. "I've never sailed on any ship before," he answered. "I've always been a get-there-as-fast-as-possible sort of person. Hold it, Miss Grant."

Caitlin stopped in her tracks and turned to stare at the man, wondering why he had given such an imperious command—and why she had obeyed it without hesitation.

He thrust out his hand to clasp hers in a firm grip. "I have you at a disadvantage. Obviously, I overheard your name at the check-in counter, but you don't know mine. I'm Mike Harris. And you were about to overshoot D stairway. Not a major problem, but why complicate matters for yourself?"

Her sentiments exactly, Caitlin thought as she managed to fix him with an unblinking stare despite the heat that was flowing into her body again. She had to remember to avoid this man's touch in the future. It did strange things to her. "Nice to meet you," she murmured, looking into his blue-gray eyes and feeling as if she'd been caught in a whirlpool. Or perhaps a riptide. Something quick and powerful. Perilous.

Mike cleared his throat and gave himself a mental shake. "You're just one flight up, and so am I. Why don't I see you to your cabin, since it's not far from mine? I have the feeling that unless someone does escort you, you're liable to end up in the hold," he added with a teasing smile, determined to keep things light.

Though Caitlin had decided in advance of her first solo trip to be more cautious than usual with strangers—especially in New York and London—she found herself nodding. She blamed Mike's disarmingly lopsided grin; it was creating odd little flips and jumps in the pit of her stomach. Anyway, she wasn't really in New York, she told herself. She was in a floating village, population just under three thousand, counting the crew.

"How do you know your way around so well?" she asked after Mike had guided her up the stairs and right to her door.

"I studied the map of the ship," he said offhandedly.

Caitlin thought she heard a note of disapproval in his tone, as if he would like to add that anyone who boarded the vessel without having done the proper homework deserved to get lost. "You actually relate all those little lines and squares to the ship itself?" she asked in amazement.

Mike couldn't help laughing. "How are you with road maps, Miss Grant?"

"Not too great," she confessed. "Hopeless, actually."

"Hopeless? That must lead to some interesting travels."

"Oh, it does," Caitlin said with a smile. "You'd be amazed what wonderful treasures there are on the wrong highways and byways."

Her words brought Mike up short. "I wouldn't know," he admitted aloud. "I've never taken the road less traveled unless I planned it in advance."

"How sad," Caitlin said thoughtfully, more to herself than to him. "I'd hate my travels—or my life—to be that predictable."

Mike frowned. He thought of his life as well

organized, not predictable. Predictable? Was that the word that had been nagging at him recently? He bristled.

The pensive silence made Caitlin regret her impulsive remark. Aware that some people—including herself lately—considered her a hopeless flake, she didn't think she was qualified to comment on anyone else's existence. "I'm glad you came along when you did," she went on much too brightly, trying to make up for her gaffe. "Otherwise I might never have found my way. I could've ended up haunting the corridors of the *QE2* forever, the resident poltergeist looking in vain for D stairway. Thanks for your help, Mr. Harris."

"Mike," he corrected her, wondering even as he spoke why he was being so friendly. "Shipmates ought to be on a first-name basis, don't you think?" Sighing inwardly in defeat, he decided there was no point in battling the warmth this female seemed to arouse in him. He might as well relax and enjoy it, since he seemed to have lost control of his impulses anyway.

"You already know my first name," Caitlin said. "I trust you'll use it."

Mike grinned. "I'll bet you hate being called Kate."

"I loathe it. And I'll bet you detest being called Michael."

Mike reached past Caitlin and pushed open the door to her stateroom. "I thought I did, but now I'm not so sure," he said with a bemused smile, his eyes once again boring into hers, his voice an intimate caress that sent shivers of unbidden excitement through her. "Somehow I like the way you make it sound."

Caitlin wondered how she could be standing safely on the deck of one of the world's largest ships and yet feel as if she'd plunged into deep, dangerous waters. "How did you know the door would open?" she asked with a strained smile, trying to keep the conversation harmless. "I just realized that I didn't get a key, and it didn't occur to me to ask."

"The key should be in the room," Mike answered. "I guess you missed that bit of information the fellow back at the check-in counter gave you."

Another flush swept over Caitlin's cheeks. She suspected she'd missed a lot of what the check-in agent had said. Mike Harris must think she was a total idiot. Maybe she was.

He surprised her with a roguish wink. "See you later, Caitlin Grant," he said as she stepped into her cabin.

Not unless she really was a flake and an idiot, Caitlin answered silently after she'd closed the door and leaned back on it, as if to keep him from forcing his way in—a laughable idea, considering what a perfect gentleman he seemed to be.

Yet Mike Harris already had invaded her stateroom, Caitlin realized. And he was likely to stay there unless she could find a way to banish him from her thoughts.

Two

Mike did a quick perusal of the information kit in his room and saw that the dining-room staff wasn't slated to be available to discuss last-minute seating reservations until almost sailing time around four. Deciding not to take any chances, he went straight up to the Queen's Grill anyway, and found the restaurant manager immediately.

The man introduced himself as Derek, and assumed a regretful expression that seemed sincere. "I'm very sorry, sir," Derek said. "We did receive your request for a table for one, but we're unable to accommodate you. Perhaps a table for two?"

A table for two could be disastrous, Mike thought. A personality conflict could make for a lot of boring or even unpleasant meals. And yet . . . "Do you have a Miss Grant listed for this dining room?" he asked, musing that he should be getting used to these surprises he kept springing on himself. It was as if the real Mike Harris had stepped aside and was watching an imposter take over his life.

Derek looked crestfallen. "Unfortunately, sir, not ten minutes ago I was asked to assign Miss Grant to a table for two with a Mr. Ralph Rush."

Mike scowled. It hadn't occurred to him that Caitlin might be meeting someone. "Did Miss Grant make the request?" he found himself asking.

"Actually, it was Mr. Rush," Derek answered, then hesitated before going on. "I'm not sure Miss Grant is aware of the arrangement. We were given her name with no seating preference attached, so I assumed she wouldn't mind if we acceded to the gentleman's request." His forehead creased as he studied his notes. "Now, we do have another single lady, a Miss . . . Miss Bunny Cantrell."

Bunny, Mike repeated silently. "How about a large group?" he suggested. He wasn't interested in ladies named Bunny. He wasn't interested in any ladies. He'd asked about Caitlin only because of a stupid, temporary urge, and he was grateful to Ralph Rush for beating him to the draw— though it rankled him to be beaten to anything. "Do you happen to have a party of at least six, with room for one more?"

Stroking his chin, Derek consulted his seating chart. "As a matter of fact, there are two eight-place tables with only three couples at each."

Mike glanced at the chart and pointed to one of the spots Derek had indicated. "That table will be fine," he said, deciding that things were looking up. If he couldn't sit alone, he could get lost in a crowd.

But as he watched Derek pencil in his name, he wondered why he had chosen the table that was right next to the one assigned to Ralph Rush and Caitlin Grant.

When he walked into the Queen's Grill just after

seven-thirty, Mike's glance went straight to Caitlin's table.

The plaid-jacketed giggler from the pier lineup was sitting there by himself. Obviously, Caitlin didn't know the man, and just as obviously Ralph Rush had zeroed in on her as a dinner partner after he'd been entertained by her embarrassment at the check counter.

Taking a chair at his own table, Mike hoped his six dinner partners would be late arrivals. For a little while he could have the large table to himself.

He couldn't resist a glance at Ralph Rush. Rush seemed nervous—or eager—constantly glancing toward the dining-room entrance, then at his watch, then at his reflection in the silver-service plate in front of him as he smoothed the sides of his outdated reddish pompadour.

As the minutes ticked toward eight, then eight-thirty, Ralph was starting on his fourth martini without having ordered dinner, and Mike was beginning to wonder where Caitlin was. Probably she'd got lost, he thought with a fondness that disturbed him more than any reaction he'd had to the woman since first seeing her on the pier.

To his mild disappointment, the three couples who were his table partners arrived and began introducing themselves, so Mike gave his name, stood up to shake hands all around and exchange the usual pleasantries, then sat down again and hoped he wouldn't be called upon for much more. He was no good at small talk.

After hearing a round of boastful chatter about rewarding professions and exclusive neighborhoods and stock-market killings, Mike braced himself for the inevitable question. He didn't have to wait long. "What do you do, Mike?"

He'd learned early in life what an awkward moment an unimpressive answer could inspire, and the fact that he could lay claim to a respectable career didn't change his feelings. Besides, he wanted to blend into the background for as long as possible. Soon enough his companions would know who he was, and if things ran true to form, he'd be bombarded with questions and thinly veiled requests for advice.

"Funny you should ask," he said, unable to resist a bit of a put-on. He tried to project the kind of naive eagerness he'd heard in his father's voice so many times during the rough years, when Stu Harris had been long on ideas and short on cash. "You see, I've got this deal going, a terrific ground-floor opportunity for investors, something I've been trying to get off the ground for a while. . . ." As he droned on without really saying anything substantial, he watched several sets of eyes glaze over and saw the members of his small audience turn their attention elsewhere.

Mike was surprised to find himself mildly depressed instead of gratified by the success of his act. Suddenly, he felt as if he actually were his father, desperately trying to convince the money men that a workable idea should be as valid a currency as cash.

Reminding himself that those days were over, that he'd had the satisfaction of watching the fruits of his own success help his dad achieve a dream and be vindicated at last, Mike decided to turn his attention to something pleasant. Someone pleasant.

Caitlin Grant.

He scowled. Where the devil was she? And why the devil did he keep watching for her?

Finally, she breezed into the restaurant, looking slightly harried and utterly beautiful, a turquoise dress hugging her modest but appealing curves and stopping a few inches above her knees, her fabulous legs still bare and glowing with a golden sheen.

Alarmed by the primitive sensuality Caitlin aroused in him, Mike tried to banish his stray thoughts. But as she drew close and he caught a whiff of a perfume as fresh and elusive as summer sweet grass, his erotic imagination went wild.

When Caitlin saw Mike, she completely forgot that she was supposed to be following Derek to her table, every sensible thought driven from her mind by the way the now-familiar gray-blue eyes were darkening to smoky charcoal.

He stood to greet her, a gesture so automatic, he seemed surprised to find himself on his feet. Caitlin was beginning to realize that Mike Harris really was a hopelessly old-fashioned gentleman, and in pearl-gray slacks, a salt-and-pepper silk-tweed blazer, and a white sport shirt, he was even more attractive than she'd allowed herself to remember. She smiled calmly at him. "Hi, Mike," she said, her voice softer and huskier than she'd intended.

He struggled to maintain the polite but detached manner he'd decided to adopt toward Caitlin. "You finally got here," he said, adding with a hint of a smile. "I was beginning to consider sending out a search party."

As she gazed at him, Caitlin knew that in spite of her lectures about being sensible, she'd been hoping he would turn out to be her table partner for the voyage. But he was seated with three couples. "You seem surprised that I managed to find my way," she said with a lift of her chin, determined to play it cool.

Then a thought hit her. Mike had been considering sending out a search party? Had he been watching for her? Waiting for her to arrive?

As he saw her expression soften and her lips curve in a sudden smile, Mike realized what his remark had revealed. He felt like a fool. "Admit it, Caitlin," he said, trying to recover lost ground by teasing her a little. "You hired a guide."

Her eyes twinkled. "All right, I confess. I left my cabin nearly half an hour ago. After my third tour of the wrong deck I started asking the crew for directions. One of them took pity on me and brought me right to the door."

And probably hopes to take you to the crew bar later, Mike added silently, his possessiveness startling him. He laughed quietly, shaking his head, pretending despair over Caitlin's tendency to get lost. "Didn't you try checking the diagrams and directories on the wall near the elevator on each deck?"

"As a matter of fact, I was about to strike out in search of this place without checking the directories," Caitlin admitted. "But the thought of you and your command of the ship's geography shamed me into being more sensible, and it was amazing. There it was in black and white! The Queen's Grill was on the boat deck. So simple!"

Mike couldn't help being flattered by her admission that he'd inspired her to try to plan her route. "So what happened?" he asked with a grin.

Caitlin rolled her eyes and launched into a convoluted explanation of how she'd ended up on the quarterdeck, wandering back and forth on that level before realizing her mistake. "What really threw me," she said at last, "is that there's a Queen's Room down there as well as the Queen's Grill up here. I ask you, is that fair? By the time I'd caught on to that little trick, I was completely baffled."

Mike had listened to her tale in rapt wonder. How anyone could get so mixed up was beyond him, but that question didn't seem particularly relevant at the moment. Nothing seemed relevant but Caitlin's lovely voice and her expressive eyes and the coil of desire inside him. "All at once I'm pretty baffled myself," he murmured.

Caitlin realized she was keeping Derek waiting while she chattered nonsensically to Mike, falling under his spell again. "I'd better get to my table," she said quietly. She turned and was startled to see that Derek was holding out a chair right behind her.

Then she saw the dinner companion she'd been assigned. He was wearing—along with one of the most dreadful blazers she'd ever seen—a Cheshire cat grin.

Mike sat down as the florid-faced man at Caitlin's table noisily pushed back his chair to stand, chuckling for no apparent reason as he thrust out his hand to her.

As Caitlin accepted his clammy grip, she caught an overpowering whiff of a cloying men's cologne—something undoubtedly called Stud or its equivalent—mingled with the aroma of a great deal of alcohol.

Her heart sank.

"Ralph Rush, at your service," the man was saying, leaning over the table as if to speak confidentially. "Rush is the name and rush is definitely the game, but don't be worried, pretty lady. I'm not gonna give you too much of a rush, though I admit I hightailed it up here this afternoon and made sure I nailed down a table with you." Ralph favored Caitlin with an exaggerated wink and seemed blissfully unaware that he was slurring his words. "So, hey, if I get carried away and move too fast for you, pretty lady, just slap

me down, and I promise to put on the brakes."
He chortled contentedly.

Caitlin managed a feeble smile as she retrieved
her hand and sank into her chair, looking up at
Derek with a brief how-could-you-do-this-to-me
glance and earning a tiny wince of apology. When
Derek had moved away, Caitlin gave the man
opposite her a puzzled look. "Did you say you
asked to be seated with me? But . . . but how
. . .? Do I know you from somewhere, Mr. Rush?"

"First, let's get you a cocktail. What'll it be? I'm
a vodka martini man myself. Shaken, of course,
not stirred." With what he seemed to think was
a cool Sean Connery half-grin, Ralph snapped his
fingers to summon a passing waiter.

Trying not to cringe, Caitlin politely asked the
waiter for a glass of mineral water and hoped he
would forgive her for the rudeness of her partner.

"Mineral water?" Ralph said as the young man
left. "Cheap date!" He guffawed. "Just kidding.
Now, listen, what's with this Mr. Rush business?
Call me Ralphie! And you don't know me unless
you happened to look over your shoulder in the
check-in line down on the pier." He gave her yet
another wink, this one bordering on a leer. "You
looked so cute when you landed flat on your dig-
nity. I told myself I had to meet you. So here we
are, pretty lady, and I kinda think we make a cute
couple. It's you and me, for five whole days."

"Here we are," Caitlin echoed in a small voice.
She'd finally recognized Ralph's chuckle. Mike
Harris had helped her when she'd dropped her
purse. Ralph Rush had laughed. And Ralph was
her dinner partner. Not Mike. She gulped. "You
and me," she said in a monotone. "For five . . .
whole . . . days."

Listening to every word, Mike had to suppress
a smile. He tried not to be too pleased. What dif-

ference did it make to him that Caitlin didn't seem thrilled by her table partner?

No difference at all, he told himself. None whatsoever.

"So how about it, Kate?" Ralph asked over dessert. "What do you say we head for the dance floor in the Theater Bar? We'll give the band a couple of shake-'em-and-bake-'em requests, let loose, and show 'em how it's done. Then we can hit the casino—I'm feelin' real lucky tonight."

Caitlin managed a polite smile, though she was seething with frustration. She'd listened to Ralph's noisily slurped soup and watched him shovel in his food while reciting his life story. And now he wanted her to go wild with him on the dance floor? Then watch him do his James Bond impersonation at the blackjack table?

She sighed inwardly, not wanting to be too hard on the man. Ralph wasn't a bad person. But she just couldn't take any more of him tonight. Unless she chose to skip eating or order room service in her cabin, she would have to cope with him for the rest of the trip, but she drew the line at joining him outside the Queen's Grill if she could help it. "I'm sorry, but I seem to have a bit of a headache," she said quite honestly.

"Aw, c'mon, Kate. A headache? That's the oldest one in the book! Change your mind. You'll be glad you did."

"Thank you anyway," she said. She really did have a nasty headache, she realized as one hand instinctively went to the back of her neck where the muscles felt as if they'd seized up like the engine of an overworked tugboat. "I think I'll just take a walk on deck and then turn in," she said.

Ralph's eyes lighted up, and she tried to back-track. "I mean, I . . . I . . ."

All at once, to Caitlin's astonishment, Mike Harris was standing beside the table and scowling down at her. "Caitlin, did you have red wine with your dinner?"

She stared at him. "No," she said, wondering if the sea air had made everyone slightly crazy. "But what . . . why . . . ?"

"Then something else must be affecting you," Mike interrupted. He turned to Ralph. "I'm sorry to butt in this way, but if we don't catch these migraines of Caitlin's right at the beginning, she's out of action for a week."

Ralph gave Mike a dubious frown. "Who're you, fella?"

Mike feigned a look of surprise at Caitlin, then returned his attention to Ralph. "Didn't she tell you? I'm her doctor. I specialize in headache control, and by the look of this woman it's a happy coincidence I'm aboard to take care of her." He held out his hand to Caitlin. "Now come on, young lady. Taking two aspirins and calling me in the morning won't do for this one."

In a daze Caitlin took Mike's hand and got to her feet, ready to follow him anywhere.

"Thank you," she murmured once they were outside the restaurant and walking through the adjacent lounge. "But how did you know I needed a fast-talking Galahad?"

"I was eavesdropping," Mike confessed as he pushed open the lounge door. "A character flaw, but I can't help myself."

"In this case, I'm grateful for that particular flaw. But I'm still curious: Why did you come to the rescue?"

Mike tried to make light of his rash interference. "You seemed less than enthusiastic about enjoying Ralph's company for the rest of the evening, and you'd just made a tactical error by admitting that you wanted to go for a walk on deck. Ralph would have liked that opportunity . . ." Mike winked and added, "pretty lady." He cupped his hand under Caitlin's elbow and guided her toward another doorway, one leading outside. "Perhaps it was presumptuous, but I flattered myself that a turn or two on the deck with me might be preferable to one with my rival."

"Your what?" Caitlin said, turning to gape in renewed shock at Mike as she went through the door he was opening. Her foot hit a watertight barrier at the door's base and she pitched forward, but Mike steadied her.

"My rival," he repeated as he tucked Caitlin's arm under his and led her onto the deck for a stroll. "I tried to reserve a table with you, but Ralph had gotten there first." He breathed in deeply of the cool sea air mingled with Caitlin's sweet fragrance, then smiled, wondering if there was some drug in her perfume that loosened his tongue, and perhaps his brain as well. "Are you warm enough?" he asked. "Even in August the night air can be chilly if you're not wearing a jacket. Here, take mine." He started to shrug out of it, but Caitlin put her hand on his arm to stop him.

"I'm fine," she protested. "Please. I'm just fine. At least, I'm warm enough. But am I slow, or has the rest of the world gone into overdrive? What happened to the legendary easy pace of shipboard life? Could we back up a little? I seem to have missed some important details."

"Such as?" Mike asked, abruptly deciding to guide Caitlin toward the deck railing; walking didn't seem like a good idea when he wanted to be able to gaze into her eyes without worrying about losing his bearings.

Caitlin barely noticed that she was following Mike's lead, but when they reached a secluded spot where they could watch the moonlight tipping the ocean's dark waves with white gold and feel the caress of a gentle wind, she had to force herself to focus on the conversation. "Such as," she answered, hoping her voice didn't sound too strained, "how you came up with your inspired story at the very moment I made my tactical error." She pressed the fingers of one hand to her temple, then went on, "Such as how, or if, you plan to pose as a doctor for the remainder of the voyage."

As it occurred to Mike that he could hide behind professionalism, he let go of Caitlin's arm. "Here. Lean back against this railing while I answer you and at the same time do something about your headache."

"Mike, you can drop the act," Caitlin protested. "Ralph's nowhere in sight." But she made the mistake of meeting Mike's gaze, and his unsettling impact made her decide to take his suggestion to heart. Leaning back with her elbows on the railing, she closed her eyes and raised her face to the welcome coolness of the breeze. It struck her that she must have been crazy to consider sexy Mike Harris a safe haven from the easily resistible Ralph Rush.

"First, I didn't come up with my story after you mentioned a walk on deck," Mike said quietly, trying not to be stirred by the way Caitlin was giving herself to the sensual pleasures of the night. "It came to me during dinner, starting when your headache took hold, right about the time the waiter whisked away your roast duck." He frowned. "What was wrong with the duck, by the way? It looked terrific, but you hardly touched your meal."

Caitlin opened her eyes and tilted her head to one side, deciding it was impossible to keep up with Mike's rapid-fire mood changes and conversational switches. "Nothing was wrong. It was wonderful, but there was too much," she fibbed, not wanting to say that Ralph's dreadful table manners had killed her appetite. "How could you know precisely when my headache started?"

"I wasn't lying about being a doctor," Mike answered. "Not even about specializing in headache control, though my field is slightly broader."

Caitlin stared at him. "No kidding?"

"No kidding. You've heard of the SRDP clinics?"

"Sounds like a place where robots go to get their computers recharged," Caitlin remarked.

"You're not far off," Mike said with a quiet laugh. "A lot of corporate robots come to us when their bodies need recharging. What they usually find out is that they need complete reprogramming. SRDP stands for Stress-Related Disease Prevention. My partner and I founded a clinic in Manhattan and apparently filled a need, because we've taken on a whole lot of junior partners and expanded into a chain operation. Now, if you're satisfied with my credentials, Miss Grant, let's see whether my shipboard manner is up to the challenge of a tension headache."

Before Caitlin could protest, Mike's fingertips were on her forehead with a soothingly light touch that conspired with the impact of his nearness to make her knees go so weak, she was glad she had the ship's rail to support her.

Instant hypnosis, she thought vaguely as her eyes closed of their own accord. Wasn't she the person who'd planned to avoid Mike Harris? The one who'd vowed not to come within twenty feet of touching him or being touched by him?

All of a sudden those plans and vows were forgotten.

Mike Harris, it seemed, was a Svengali of the first order.

Three

On one level Mike was amazed that Caitlin was so trusting, yet on another he wasn't surprised at all. The two of them seemed to have zoomed in on an unexpected closeness without needing the usual preliminary steps.

He was glad when Caitlin broke the charged silence.

"So you . . ." Caitlin swallowed hard and started again, having a little trouble forming words. Mike's soothing caress was undermining all her faculties. "You have a chain of clinics specializing in the effects of stress?"

"Most of them are more general," Mike answered. "But we do put the emphasis on preventive health care. I'd rather teach a patient how not to invite heart disease than recommend a triple bypass, and all the people who work at our clinics share that philosophy." Touching three fingers of each hand to the center of Caitlin's forehead and exerting slight pressure as he made outward sweeping motions above her brows, he spoke quietly. "To get back to the question of how I knew when your headache started, Caitlin, I saw two little furrows appear at this spot. Nobody should have those furrows on the first evening of an ocean voyage. We're going to have to do something about the cause—or causes."

Caitlin was too caught up in a languorous trance to protest.

Mike moved his fingers to her temples and made slow, pain-erasing circles, at the same time stroking her brows with his thumbs. After several moments he cradled her face between his palms. "Let go," he said quietly. "The muscles of your jaw are tense. In fact, all your facial muscles are tight. Release them, Caitlin. Inhale slowly, exhale, that's it." He was tempted to lower his mouth to Caitlin's as he watched her lips soften and part slightly, but he reminded himself that he was concerned about her headache, not trying to start something he had no intention of finishing.

Yet every muscle in his body clenched in inverse proportion to Caitlin's increasing level of relaxation, and he focused more and more on her inviting lips, intrigued by the upward tilt at their corners, drawn by the sweetness he could almost taste. And her skin was such a pleasure to touch, so soft and cool and silky. . . .

He let his hands slide downward to surround the column of her throat, his fingers massaging the rigid sinews at the back of her neck.

"That's wonderful," Caitlin murmured as Mike unerringly found and worked out the kinks and tension spots she hadn't even realized were there.

"Shh, don't talk," he said just above a whisper. "Talking's an effort. Your job right now is to stop making any effort. Drop your arms to your sides. . . ." He waited until she'd obeyed him, then went on softly, "Just let go, Caitlin. Listen to the swishing sound of the ship sliding through the water. Feel the slight vibration under your feet and let it move through your whole body. Breathe in the salty tang of the air. Relax, think pleasant thoughts . . ."

Pleasant thoughts, Caitlin repeated silently. How could she think any other kind? And with Mike's hands performing magic, how could she keep them from becoming *too* pleasant?

Mike was having his own problems. As he began massaging Caitlin's shoulders, still gazing at her mouth, he found her allure harder and harder to resist. "Turn around," he said, more brusquely than he intended.

Caitlin's eyes flew open, and she frowned, but Mike's strong fingers merely put pressure on her shoulders in just the right way to make her do as he'd said. She turned around so her back was to him. Odd, she thought. Nobody ever told her what to do—not successfully, at any rate. If anyone tried, she usually just laughed. She'd had to learn independence at an early age; she'd learned well. She was her own person, and planned to stay that way.

So why, she asked herself, was she so docile with Mike Harris?

He started working on her shoulders, his thumbs finding and soothing knots of tension there and at the top of her spine. "You're a mess," he muttered.

"Why, thank you, sir—my first shipboard compliment," Caitlin said, wondering why the timbre of Mike's voice had sharpened again. Suddenly edgy, she started to move away, but his fingers exerted their persuasive pressure again, and she stayed where she was, watching the way the huge ship sliced through the ocean's waves and musing that Mike had been doing the same to her defenses until he'd altered the mood so abruptly, his voice and manner not at all like his gentle hands. But she was glad he'd changed. She didn't want her control pierced.

"Take advantage of the ship's spa for the next few days," Mike said, deliberately sounding like a dispassionate and disapproving physician snapping out orders to a difficult patient, all the while wishing the nape of Caitlin's neck hadn't turned out to be every bit as tempting as her lips. "Take some aerobic dance classes, soak in a hot tub, book a massage. You get headaches regularly, don't you?"

Scowling, Caitlin mumbled, "Yes, but not always bad ones." She added pointedly, "Certainly not migraines that put me out of action for a week."

"Count yourself lucky," Mike shot back. "But I'll bet you're plagued by at least low-level discomfort most of the time."

Caitlin didn't answer.

Mike found more knots in Caitlin's back. They made him strangely annoyed, and his voice showed it. "Judging by the way you picked at your meal tonight, I'd venture to say you don't eat properly, which is one sure way to guarantee chronic headaches. Are you a fashion model, by any chance?"

"Sometimes," Caitlin answered testily, wondering when she had agreed to an impromptu physical and cross-examination.

"I thought so," he said, not realizing how clipped his words sounded, how angry. His mind was on another model, an eighteen-year-old beauty whose parents had dragged her to the Manhattan clinic in a desperate attempt to find out why she was starving herself to death. A determined staff—including a particularly gifted psychiatrist—had saved that girl, but Mike had seen too many of those cases, especially during his intern and residency years in hospital emergency wards. Was Caitlin a candidate for that kind of self-destruction? He didn't think so—not with her radiant glow. Still, she clearly didn't take proper care of herself. "What's wrong with women anyway?" he demanded. "Does being thin really mean more to you than staying healthy? Than life itself?"

"So you're saying I'm skinny?" Caitlin said with a surge of annoyance. Mike had hit on a more sensitive spot with his words than with his fingers, transporting her back in an instant to a humiliating adolescence when her soul-numbing loneliness had been made all the more difficult because she'd been too tall and thin, an angular-faced Olive Oyl with no Popeye to laugh away her self-doubt—or to punch out the Blutos, which she'd wanted to do more than once. Why did otherwise reasonable people seem to believe that comments about weight were acceptable when they wouldn't dream of making cracks about a misshapen nose or a large facial birthmark?

She shook herself free and turned to face Mike, for some reason choosing to explode at him, though she'd spent a lifetime smiling and pretending to let hurtful remarks roll off her. "So what you're saying, Dr. Harris, is that I'm a scrawny reed. A human clothes hanger. No curves, no womanliness. And if that's not bad enough, I'm a mass of tension who can't find her way from point A to point B without making several unscheduled detours." She was embarrassed to be working herself into such a snit, but couldn't seem to help it. Vaguely, she wondered if she was just trying to distance herself from Mike because he was getting to her on too many levels, in ways she simply wouldn't allow. "Why on earth are you wasting any time at all with me?" she heard herself snapping. "Are you a workaholic? Compulsive about healing the world? About teaching the rest of us to get organized? About telling us all the ways we should be more sensible?"

"Yes. No!" Mike said, then stared in shock at Caitlin Grant. Never in his adult life had he given an answer that was anything but final and unambiguous. Never had he reacted with instant defensiveness to anything said to him by anyone.

And never had he been tempted so sorely by a woman's mouth. "I didn't say you were scrawny, or even skinny," he pointed out, determined not to let Caitlin Grant undermine his self-control, yet at the same time puzzled. Why was she so angry at him? "I said you're a mess, and in terms of tension you are. I also said you probably don't eat properly, and I'll still put down odds that you don't. But for the record, I happen to think you're gorgeous, and I'd be a lot more comfortable if you were a little less womanly. It just drives me crazy to see otherwise intelligent human beings willfully starving themselves, that's all. Especially when sensibly nutritious food doesn't have to lead to weight gain."

Now he was delivering a lecture, he thought disgustedly, then found himself going right on with it. "Did you hear me, Miss Grant? I said you're gorgeous. I meant it. And you'd be exactly as gorgeous if you fleshed out those fantastic bones of yours a little. And the reason I'm wasting time with you, as you put it, is . . . well, it's beyond me. Because you're trouble, Caitlin Grant, the kind of trouble I've avoided for a very long time. If I had any sense, I'd stay as far from you as possible. But there's one problem. . . ." All at once the self-control he'd always been able to count on deserted him. It simply disappeared. Nothing remained but an urgent need. "This problem," he said, hauling her into his arms and taking the kiss he'd been craving since the first moment he'd laid eyes on the woman.

Caitlin's shocked gasp was lost in the cognac-scented recesses of Mike's mouth. Too sudden, she thought dizzily. Too fast, too unexpected. How could she fight? How could she escape arms that were crushing her, strong fingers that were tangled in her hair, lips that were moving over hers so mercilessly? So deliciously? What could she do about a tongue that boldly parted her lips and delved into her mouth as if rightfully exploring and taking? Her own arms were collaborating with her captor, creeping around him and clinging desperately. Her treacherous body was pressing against the hard male form it ought to be resisting. Her mouth, in fact her whole being, was opening to this invasion with eagerness.

Then, just as abruptly as the sweet assault had begun, it ended.

"Dammit!" Mike said as he thrust Caitlin away from him. "I don't do this kind of thing!"

Trembling, Caitlin struggled for a breath. "And just how did I inspire such a dramatic first?"

Mike searched her eyes for several long moments, then raked his fingers through his hair. "Beats the hell out of me," he said at last, stunned that he, Mike Harris, a reasonable and sane man, unfailingly and carefully liberated, respectful of women's equality and autonomy, had reverted to the courting techniques of a cave dweller. "Maybe I'd better let Ralph have you after all," he murmured, then stared at Caitlin, realizing only at that moment that he'd been toying almost subconsciously with the insane idea of trying to talk her dinner companion into trading places with him.

Caitlin's eyes widened and flashed brilliant

green flames as sheer outrage shot through her. "Maybe you'd better let Ralph *have* me? As if I'm yours to hand over to him! Well, let me tell you what's up, Doc. You can stick your Neanderthal attitude in your stethoscope! I don't appreciate being treated like the prize in a contest between you and Call-Me-Ralphie, and I'll pick at my food and dine with a person of my own choosing and stay as skinny as I please, thank you very much. And what's more, I'm beginning to think the air's too thin on the upper deck—"

"The boat deck," Mike automatically put in, then winced. It didn't seem like a good time to be correcting Caitlin on her shipboard geography. When she looked at him as if he'd lost his own upper deck, he added lamely, "This is the boat deck. I . . . I just . . . thought you should know."

Caitlin gave her head a shake as if to clear it. "The air *is* too thin. Maybe I should ask to be downgraded to the restaurant I was booked into to begin with." She tried to push past Mike to head for her room.

His arm shot out as if of its own accord and stopped her, then pulled her against him. "I'm not sure where to begin apologizing," he said, wrapping his other arm around her and ignoring her struggle to free herself. "Obviously, I've been a total bumbler. Please don't change dining rooms, Caitlin. I'd miss you. Don't ask me to explain, because I can't. I've never acted this way before. But it's only fair for you to let me spend the next few days proving I'm not always the raving fool you've seen tonight." Crooking his index finger under her chin and lifting, Mike managed a perplexed smile. "If I can get Ralph to vacate his chair at your table, may I take his place?"

Caitlin's pride and sense told her to do everything in her power to avoid Mike's charm, but she couldn't. Just couldn't. "Why is it only fair?" she asked in what she knew was token resistance.

For once, Mike had no answer. "I don't know. Give me a minute—I'll think of something."

Beginning to realize she was disturbing Mike as much as he was upsetting her, Caitlin reached up and touched her hand to his cheek. She wasn't surprised to feel that his muscles, like hers, were anything but relaxed. "While you're thinking, Mike, perhaps you should consider this question: Do you really want to spend the next few days proving something to a woman you probably won't ever see again after we reach Southampton?"

Mike didn't know what to say. Caitlin was right. Yet her words left him feeling unbelievably bleak. Never to see her again? He couldn't imagine it—which didn't make any sense at all.

He frowned. Perhaps his mind had snapped.

Caitlin leaned forward to kiss his other cheek. "I think I'll call it a night; I flew in from Florida yesterday and tried to munch too big a piece of the Big Apple in one night. I'm pretty tired."

"You're from Florida?" Mike said for no particular reason except to keep her from leaving.

"No. I was living there, though."

" 'Was'? Not anymore?"

Caitlin smiled and steeled herself to leave before the conversation became too friendly. She'd been caught off guard once; she didn't plan to let it happen again. "Maybe, maybe not. I'm a gypsy. But right now I really must say good night."

"I'll see you to your cabin," Mike offered.

"Trust me," Caitlin answered. "I can find my way." Gently and reluctantly, she extricated herself from his arms and moved away from him, heading for the doorway to go inside.

Halfway there, she stopped and turned to smile at him. "By the way, Dr. Harris, thanks."

He raised one brow quizzically. "For what?"

Caitlin tried a Ralphie wink. "My headache's gone."

By one-thirty of the second day of the voyage, Mike was on pins and needles.

Not only was he wondering why Caitlin hadn't shown up for breakfast or lunch, he had inherited Ralph Rush, who kept leaning over and trying to get in on what he seemed to perceive as the action at the larger table.

"Hey, why don't I be straight with you, Doc?" Ralph suddenly said to Mike in a low voice. "I been keepin' my ears open here, and the way I see it, I got a lot in common with the movers and shakers you're sittin' with. I don't suppose you'd consider tradin' places, would you?"

Mike turned to gape at Ralph. "I thought you wanted to sit with Caitlin."

"Hell, what good's a no-show broad with a migraine? Anyway, Kate's not exactly a live wire, if you get my drift." Ralph cleared his throat, obviously noting Mike's scowl and realizing his sales technique needed some polishing. "What I mean to say is, wouldn't it be a good idea for you to be close by if she ever does show up? You bein' her doctor and all, shouldn't you keep an eye on her?"

Although Mike had decided during a restless night that he should stay as far from Caitlin as possible, he was tempted. After all, what could be wrong with having an attractive table companion? Surely, he had enough control to be able to enjoy her company for the next few days without letting things get out of hand.

Yet just as he was opening his mouth to accept Ralph's offer, Mike found that his conscience wouldn't let him do it. He knew what Ralph was after, and the man was being naive. Just like Stu Harris. The memories of his father's elusive dreams and dashed hopes were too vivid; Mike couldn't sit back and watch Ralph make a fool of himself. "Ralph, I know you've been listening to these fellows bragging about their investment successes," he said bluntly, "and I'm pretty sure you're hoping to interest them in some project, but I don't think it'll happen. At best they'll cut you down and make you feel like a lowlife. At worst they'll pick your brains, then take your ideas and run with them."

Ralph rolled his eyes. "You been burned too, huh?"

"Indirectly," Mike said with an edge of bitterness he'd never been able to shake completely, even though he knew his own drive and determination, and therefore his success, were a direct result of his father's humiliations.

"Yeah, well, I learned from my scars," Ralph said with a gleam in his eyes that all at once made him seem less of a buffoon. "Look, Doc, I don't need your permission to sit at that table. There's room for eight, remember? I could just decide to move over there. The thing is, I wouldn't want to hurt Kate's feelings by leavin' her alone. She's a nice girl, if you like the skinny intellectual type. But I got my eye on this sexy blonde across the room, name's Bunny or something cute like that—"

"You win," Mike said, abruptly deciding that Ralph was on his own. "Starting at dinner tonight?"

"Good man," Ralph said with one of his more

subtle winks. "And you take care of Kate, hear? Funny, I feel kinda responsible for her."

Caitlin seemed to have a way of arousing that feeling in people, Mike mused as he got up and left the dining room. He couldn't stop wondering about her: Had she skipped both meals, or had she gone for the Lido buffet? Had Ralph Rush driven her from the Queen's Grill? Or had Mike Harris done it? Had she asked for a transfer to another dining room? Was she lost? *Did* she have a migraine?

Lecture notes, Mike thought desperately. He could go over the points he wanted to cover in his shipboard lecture. And he could give his London speech another polishing. Then there was the background information about the British clinics he'd been invited to tour.

He scowled. Was he a worse workaholic than any of his patients?

No, he decided firmly. He just had a lot of energy to burn, a lineup of stupid questions and confused thoughts he wanted driven from his mind, and a low boredom threshold.

To salve his conscience about not relaxing on the voyage as he'd promised the entire Manhattan clinic staff he would, he changed from slacks to shorts when he reached his cabin, made a quick ship-to-shore call to his secretary to make sure everything on the home front was under control, then stuffed his notes into a small portfolio and took them with him to a deck chair in the sun.

By four o'clock he'd had his fill of fresh air. He decided to continue going over his papers in the comfort of his cabin, where the sun wouldn't glare off the pages.

He took a shortcut through the Grand Lounge, his mind wandering back to Caitlin Grant. The more he fought her presence in his thoughts, it seemed, the more she dominated them. He was only dimly aware of a voice droning over the lounge's public-address system and of a group of passengers, mostly females, sitting in rapt attention, their eyes focused on the stage area.

He followed their gazes and stopped dead.

Caitlin was pirouetting, showing off the floaty skirt of a strapless, classically draped rose chiffon gown.

Mike sank into the nearest empty chair and watched her flash her brilliant smile, finding himself checking to see whether her charm was directed at anyone in particular. Any other man.

This situation was turning serious, he thought vaguely. Mike Harris, jealous? What next?

There was no escaping it. Every time Caitlin glanced into the audience and seemed to make eye contact, Mike was seized by an irresistible compulsion to know where she was looking.

It occurred to him to wonder how Caitlin happened to be appearing in the ship's fashion show. He'd seen the event mentioned on the day's schedule, but hadn't paid much attention except to notice that the models were supposed to be the dancers from the nighttime cabaret. Caitlin's name hadn't been listed, so obviously she'd been brought in at the last minute.

The dark mood he realized he'd been battling all day suddenly lifted a little. Perhaps Caitlin hadn't asked to be assigned to another restaurant. Maybe she wasn't avoiding him. Probably she'd been busy rehearsing all day.

She was a first-rate model, he thought as her long, easy strides brought her close to where he was sitting. Confident and breezy and natural, no stiff movements, no apparent self-consciousness. Dynamite.

Mike's body responded accordingly. Memories

of the way she'd felt in his arms the night before added fuel to the fires that had been doing a slow burn inside him ever since. The sweet taste and soft yielding of her mouth came back to him with an almost palpable force that fanned the hot coals until they were ready to burst into flame.

Caitlin saw him, and her smile faltered just a little, then brightened.

Mike wasn't sure how to interpret that reaction, and his confusion was just another symptom of the Caitlin Grant syndrome that seemed to have gripped him. He prided himself on his expertise at reading body language. The flicker of an eyelash could tell him secrets he wasn't supposed to know. The clenching of a hand, the tremor of a lip, the averted glance—his stock-in-trade.

Yet he couldn't read Caitlin at all.

He stayed through to the end of the fashion show, and never did decide whether Caitlin's smile had a special warmth when she trained it on him. But he applauded enthusiastically along with the rest of the audience when Jonathan Collins, the cruise director, made a point of thanking her for helping out in a pinch.

Mike was doubly impressed by Caitlin's performance as he listened to Collins explain how the manager of the ship's boutique had spotted her in the shop in the morning, just after learning that one of the dancer-models was under the weather. Caitlin had agreed to fill in. "Sounds like fun," was all she'd apparently said. And she'd made it look like fun.

When the applause died down, Caitlin was backstage somewhere with the other models, so Mike headed for the on-board florist shop, ordered a spray of bright summer flowers, wrote out a card, and asked that the bouquet be sent to Caitlin's stateroom on the double.

Only when he was back in his own cabin did it occur to him that such a gesture was as uncharacteristic of Mike Harris as just about everything else he'd been doing since Caitlin Grant had stepped up to the check-in counter on the pier in New York.

Four

Mike stood near the bronze bust of England's reigning monarch in the Queen's Room, listening absently to the music of the dance band at the far end of the huge lounge and trying to believe he just happened to have stationed himself near the entrance to the captain's cocktail party. No special reason.

Sipping champagne, he kept his edginess at bay by watching the stilted poses people struck as the ship's photographer snapped their self-conscious smiles for posterity and profit.

After his body had suffered its third overdose of adrenaline because someone vaguely resembling Caitlin had walked into the lounge, Mike had to admit he was watching for her, waiting for her, wishing she would show up.

Yet he was mystified. What *was* it about the woman? Why did she haunt him? Why couldn't he see just a lovely color and shape when he looked into her eyes, instead of glimpsing a hidden vulnerability that touched his heart? And why did he sense a unique kind of serenity in

Caitlin, an answer to some secret need within him?

He was so deep in thought, he gave a visible start when Caitlin finally walked into the room. He stopped wondering why she captivated him; she simply took his breath away. He'd thought that anything she wore after the rose chiffon of the fashion show would be an anticlimax, but she'd managed to look every bit as stunning in a dress splashed with multicolored flowers that draped her slender body in a full-length sarong style and knotted casually over one shoulder, intriguingly baring the other.

Mike watched as the photographer asked Caitlin to pause for a snapshot, and when she struck a careless pose, Mike was fascinated. Caitlin knew her body, instinctively arranging herself with no apparent effort or thought, her expertise proved by her ultimate naturalness.

Glancing around the room as soon as the photo had been taken, Caitlin spied Mike and her smile took on a sudden glow that made his heart leap to his throat. Without hesitation she moved toward him.

"Thank you for the flowers," she said as soon as she reached him. "They're beautiful. They remind me of a wild English garden, tamed just enough to be brought indoors."

Not unlike Caitlin Grant, Mike thought, but said aloud, "You were great in the show this afternoon. The people in charge must have thought some miracle had sent them a stand-in model of your caliber."

Pleased by Mike's compliments and at the same time dazzled by what his dark hair and golden tan did for a crisp white shirt and black dinner jacket, Caitlin couldn't manage more than a mumbled thanks. She'd thought she was prepared for his impact. Just before leaving her cabin, she'd vowed to remain in firm control of her emotions if she found herself talking to him, but now she wasn't sure she could handle even a few moments of conversation with Mike without stammering and blushing and generally acting like a nitwit.

As a waiter approached with champagne, Mike automatically exhibited the fierce protectiveness Caitlin seemed to inspire in him. "At the risk of annoying my newest patient again, I'm going to suggest a juice or a soft drink for you," he said with what he hoped was a disarming smile. "Unless I miss my guess, you were too busy to eat proper meals today, and drinking bubbly on an empty stomach could give you the worst kind of headache."

Caitlin started to reach for a glass of champagne just to assert herself, then realized she was being childish. She pulled back. "You're right," she conceded reluctantly. "Too bad. I guess ginger ale will have to do."

Turning to the waiter, Mike politely relayed her request, and Caitlin couldn't help contrasting his manner with Ralph Rush's finger-snapping. For perhaps the hundredth time she wished she hadn't discouraged Mike from trying to switch seats with Ralph.

"Have I mentioned that you look absolutely stunning tonight?" Mike said as he returned his attention to Caitlin.

"Thank you. Have I mentioned that you look pretty fantastic yourself?" Caitlin countered.

Silence. Neither of them could think of another thing to say.

Finally, Mike heaved a deep sigh. "Well, that takes care of the pleasantries. Now what do we talk about?" He paused, then blurted out, "I'm feeling awkward with you, Caitlin. The kiss, the dumb quarrel . . . how could two strangers get under each other's skin that way?"

Caitlin stared at him for a moment, taken aback. "You certainly are direct," she said at last, then shifted to a playful approach. "But I've been pondering the problem, analyzing it as I would if I were a physician at your SRDP clinic. My diagnosis is that we're suffering from a case of OLV that can be controlled only by strong doses of ECT."

Mike's lips twitched with amusement. "I don't believe I'm familiar with the syndrome or the treatment, Dr. Grant. Would you care to explain?"

"Of course, Dr. Harris. OLV is, as you might expect, Ocean Liner Vertigo, and ECT is Extremely Clear Thinking."

"And the prognosis?" Mike asked, not sure he bought Caitlin's theory even though he wanted to believe that the little drama they were playing out was inspired simply by the romantic setting.

"An infatuation at sea is like the ship itself," Caitlin said airily, despite the way Mike's quizzical smile heated her blood. "It'll run its course and move on to its next port of call before you know it."

"I trust you're right," Mike said with exaggerated seriousness. "We both know that allowing the affliction to become chronic would be foolish, don't we?"

Caitlin nodded. "Practically fatal."

"We're not suited to each other," Mike pointed out.

Caitlin wasn't too crazy about hearing that particular truth from Mike, but she smiled. "Not at all. And our differences are much more fundamental than . . ." Searching for an analogy, she took inspiration from the song the band was playing. "Than, for instance, my saying 'tom-*ay*-to' and your saying 'tom-*ah*-to.'"

"Much more fundamental," Mike agreed, slightly surprised that Caitlin would know the words to such an old song, even a jazz standard. "One small difficulty . . ."

"Yes?" Caitlin asked, infusing the single word with unintended hope.

Mike's gaze locked on hers. "You've made an assumption that I say 'tom-*ah*-to,' when in fact I say 'tom-*ay*-to,' same as you." He smiled and added in a low, persuasive drawl, "Perhaps our other differences are equally false."

Caitlin swallowed hard. What was Mike's point? His game? After all, *he* was the one who'd said they weren't suited. "The music's great, isn't it?" she said, trying to neutralize the charged atmosphere. The waiter brought her ginger ale, and she took a cooling sip before going on—and sounding to her own ears like a total airhead. "I love the numbers they're playing. They make me think Fred is going to whirl Ginger through here any minute."

On an impulse utterly foreign to him Mike took Caitlin's glass and set it along with his own on a nearby table, ignoring her startled expression, then grabbed her by the hand, led her through the crowd to the dance floor, and turned her to face him. "I'm no Astaire, but I think I can get my feet around this one," he said, putting one arm around her waist to pull her close, then flattening his palm over the small of her back to press her against him.

"You . . . you simply have to stop doing this sort of thing!" Caitlin protested, though her body seemed to have a will of its own, instinctively fitting itself to his.

"No, Caitlin," Mike said, his lips against her ear. "*You* have to stop doing this sort of thing."

Caitlin's suddenly labored breathing made speech difficult, but she managed a small show of outrage. "Exactly what am I supposed to stop doing?"

Mike tightened his arm around her and executed a few turns before answering. "The way you look at me is one of our biggest problems—apart from the way you look, period, which is a total disaster to any man who's trying to maintain some sort of equilibrium." He raised his head to smile down at her. "But I guess that's not really your fault."

"How very tolerant of you," Caitlin said with heavy irony. But she couldn't seem to be convincingly angry.

"And that little catch in your voice—did you hear it just now?" he teased. "The touch of huskiness, the breathlessness, the excitement that's about to spill over and create havoc . . ." Mike whirled Caitlin again, then again and again, his taut thigh pressing into her, the subtle pressure of his hands guiding her, his gaze holding hers until his dark eyes were her only focal point in a spinning room.

Finally, he slowed the pace, gathering Caitlin close and trailing an arc of light kisses over the rim of her ear. "Oh, and let's have no more of these little shivers," he said as a tremor rippled through her body. "They set off sympathetic vibrations inside me that could lead to all sorts of natural catastrophes."

Startled by the searing heat spreading through her, Caitlin tried to marshal her forces to battle the effects of Mike's words, his touch, the nearness of his lips to a throbbing pulse spot just under her ear. But she was all molten, fluid desire, incapable of summoning a shred of resistance.

"That's just what I mean," Mike said with a rasp as his game began backfiring, his own control slipping thanks to the siege he'd begun so impetuously. Yet he had started it, and he couldn't retreat. "What's all this softening and yielding and feminine pliancy? You make me forget myself, Caitlin Grant. You make me forget everything." He guided her to one semiprivate corner of the small dance floor and gently nipped at her earlobe, then soothed it with his tongue before drawing back and gazing at her, releasing her hand so he could span her slender waist with his long fingers.

Caitlin vaguely noticed her arms twining around Mike's neck, and in some recess of her mind she was aware that while he had begun leading her through miniscule movements to the music, the room was still spinning, and she had to cling to him or lose her balance completely. "You're not fair," she whispered. "You're the one who starts things."

"We seem to be at an impasse," Mike said, his hands sliding down to rest on her hips as the band swung into a Latin beat, and Caitlin instinctively began swaying in response. "Neither of us is willing to take responsibility for this unusual brand of seasickness we're suffering," he went on, amazed that he could sound almost normal when the blood was pounding through his veins and there was a roaring in his ears like a wild typhoon. "Neither of us seems to be prepared to stop."

"Someone has to," Caitlin said desperately.

In the next instant someone did. "Hey-hey-*hey*, look who's here!" a familiar voice crowed from behind Mike.

Mike's gaze remained locked on Caitlin's. "Maybe if we pretend he isn't there, he'll disappear," he muttered so that only she could hear.

"I don't think so," Caitlin said in a low voice. "Ralphie isn't the disappearing type."

Mike winced as a meaty hand landed on his shoulder.

"Hey, Mikey! Kate! Glad to see you've got the migraine on the run." Ralph continued to dance absentmindedly with his heavily bejeweled, fluffy blond partner as he talked. "By the looks of things, you two are gettin' to be just a little more than doctor and patient, right? So our little deal worked out okay, huh, Doc?"

Caitlin looked questioningly at Mike.

Mike wished he'd mentioned the table switch before Ralph had blurted it out. Caitlin had made it clear she didn't like being traded as if she were a piece of property on a Monopoly board.

To make things worse, Ralph sensed an awkward moment, misunderstood it, and gave Caitlin the sheepish smile of a man who had ditched her for someone else. "Glad to see you're up and around, Kate," he said with an extra dollop of heartiness. "I guess the doc's taking good care of you, especially now that you're tablemates."

"I'm monitoring the lady very closely," Mike said, directing a teasing but anxious smile at Caitlin.

Ralph's new girlfriend beamed at Mike, patting her frizzy upsweep and giving her ample hips a languid rhumba roll despite the jazzy number the band had just switched to in its fast-paced medley. "I don't believe I've met your friends," she said in a classic chorus-girl singsong. "Howsabout an intro, Ralphie?"

"Uh-*uh*," Ralph said, playfully shaking his finger at the lady. "*You* I plan to keep all to myself, Bunny."

Bunny, Mike repeated silently. So this was Bunny. He could have had a table with her instead of with Caitlin. He smiled. Somebody up there liked him.

Deciding an escape was in order, he took Caitlin's hand in his and opened up into a jive worthy of a fifties *American Bandstand* regular. As with everything, when he'd been faced with having to learn to dance as a teenager, he'd worked diligently to master every step his good-natured mother had been able to show him. He'd turned out to be not bad. Outdated, but not bad. And to his pleased amazement, he still had the moves down pat.

Caitlin kept up, though she stared at him throughout the wild dance as if not sure how she'd ended up with a madman. The music ended, and Mike whirled her back into his arms. "You're fantastic," he said, hugging her. "Where did you learn to dance like that?"

"Here," she said, gasping for breath. "Just now. You didn't leave me much choice but to follow you—which I suspect is pretty typical of the way you operate."

Grasping her shoulders, Mike held her back so he could grin at her. "Are you angry that Ralph and I made arrangements without consulting you?"

Caitlin couldn't manage a good mad, so she just shook her head and laughed. "I'm furious. It's an insult! Ralph traded me without a qualm, but he plans to keep his Bunny all to himself."

"He was trying to do you a favor," Mike fibbed. "Somehow Ralph got the idea that you needed someone to hover over you a little, and who better than your doctor?"

Caitlin couldn't suppress her smile. As she began counting up the meals she would be sharing with Mike, every fiber of her being sang with anticipation. The docking at Southampton suddenly seemed to be soon in coming.

But just half an hour later she began to get reminders of the hidden shoals that could make for a rough voyage.

The rockiness started about halfway through the soup course, over the trivial question of why she'd been upgraded.

Caitlin still had no idea why she'd been transferred to One Deck, and Mike couldn't fathom why she wasn't more curious. "A question like that doesn't drive you crazy until you chase down the answer?" he asked with a hint of frustration in his tone.

Caitlin took a dainty sip of her almond-and-celery cream soup. There was no way she would admit she was reluctant to ask questions in case someone realized there'd been a mistake. Now that Mike was her partner for meals, she didn't want to chance being bumped back downstairs. "Why should it drive me crazy?" she asked with a smile.

Mike couldn't think of an important rational reason, but his own curiosity was piqued. "I'd have to know what wheels turned and why," he said, then had a thought. "Evidently, the public-relations department sometimes does this sort of thing for travel agents, tour-group leaders, journalists. . . ."

Caitlin's ears perked up. "Journalists?" She considered that possibility but discarded it. "You must mean big-time travel writers. I've been scribbling a little column in a small weekly paper in St. Pete's—"

"I thought you were a model," Mike interrupted. "A very professional, successful one, I might add."

Caitlin was pleased by the compliment but disturbed to find herself wishing she were as successful as Mike seemed to believe. Unaccustomed to the temptation to try to impress anyone, she downplayed and even omitted whatever genuine achievements she could boast. "I guess I'm professional in the strictest sense of the word, but I've never commanded huge fees and plum assignments."

Mike was puzzled. "Why not? You certainly have a distinctive look, and you seemed to know what you were doing in that show this afternoon."

"Like everything, an important modeling career takes a dedication I don't have. When I was sixteen, I thought I'd be the next Cheryl Tiegs, but it wasn't long before I realized I didn't want to work hard enough to make it to the big time," she said almost defiantly.

"So you switched to journalism?"

Caitlin laughed. "Heavens, no. I was registered with a temporary office help agency in St. Pete's, and I was sent to the newspaper office to fill in for their receptionist. It turned out that she quit, so I stayed on, getting very bored. Out of sheer desperation I wrote a couple of sample columns for the editor. Beauty tips, mainly, though I did some chatty pieces about other topics as well. I think there was an editorial hole that week, so my stuff was printed, and my angle was different enough to make the column catch on and become a regular feature."

Mike was sufficiently intrigued to forget about

the matter of the upgrade. "What angle did you take?"

"I targeted what our society rather awkwardly refers to as 'the mature woman.'" Caitlin answered, then frowned. "As if getting older is a slightly insensitive thing for a lady to do in a world that's dedicated to the youth cult. As you probably know, Florida tends to have a lot of mature women."

"So you became a columnist. Have you tried expanding to bigger papers, dailies perhaps? Magazines?"

"Hardly. I'm an amateur who happened to fill a need. I've kept up the column because it's fun. It certainly doesn't pay much." Caitlin thought for a moment, then added, "You know, I did write a few pieces about planning for this trip. . . ." Giving her head a little shake, she said, "But there's no way the Cunard people would have seen those columns. No, I think I got the upgrade by the luck of the draw."

Mike shook his head in despair. "Are you're satisfied with that explanation?"

"Why shouldn't I be? Such things do happen, you know."

"Then why didn't you believe it could happen to you in journalism. Or in modeling?" Mike blurted out, shocking himself by sticking his nose into someone else's private business, yet unable to stop. "Why did you give up?"

Why indeed, Caitlin thought, though she refused to admit that he'd struck a nerve. "I've never had a burning ambition to hit the cover of *Glamour* or to become some designer's pet dress form," she said bluntly. "And to cut straight to the heart of what's really bugging you about me, let me confess right here and now—though you'll be shocked and appalled—that unlike my peers"—she leaned forward and spoke in a stage whisper, managing a furtive look—"I don't care about having a glitzy career." Straightening up, she shrugged. "Anyway, how could I get serious about work I always found essentially silly? Let's face it, Mike. What you do matters, but my prancing around playing dress-up? Even writing columns about how to keep eye shadow from caking? It's all a crock."

"I take it you're independently wealthy," Mike said in a tone he couldn't keep free of sarcasm. He'd had to work too hard for whatever creature comforts he'd managed to acquire; he didn't have much patience with silver-spoon babies. And obviously, that was exactly what Caitlin Grant was.

Caitlin heard the edge in Mike's voice and saw the tightening of his jaw, and she wondered why she'd been lulled into thinking they could spend time together without coming to verbal blows. Obviously, he was arrogant enough to think everyone should share his view of life. "To start with, I'm reasonably independent, though not wealthy," she said evenly, putting down her soup spoon and looking him in the eye. "I'm not a career freak, but I do work. Jill-of-all-trades, master of none. A drifter, off to see the world, corny as it sounds. I support myself with whatever job is at hand—secretarial, sales, waitressing, or even modeling."

Mike was thoroughly mystified. In his world everyone was an overachiever. He'd never met anyone with Caitlin's take-it-as-it-comes outlook. And though it occurred to him that he was guilty of defining Caitlin by her career success—or lack of it—and was behaving exactly like all the people who infuriated him by asking the *What-do-you-do?* question and looking down on anyone offering the wrong answer, he couldn't seem to mask his disapproval. "First class on the *QE2* is a little beyond the means of a waitress or a secretary," he pointed out.

"This trip was a gift," Caitlin said, wondering why she was bothering to explain. "A bequest from my aunt. Great-aunt, actually."

"I'm sorry," Mike said, wishing he hadn't spoken out of turn. "Were you close to her?"

Caitlin stared at him in puzzlement for a moment before realizing the word she'd used. "Oh, dear," she said with a laugh. "I've misled you. My aunt is very much alive; it's just that she gave me some of my inheritance early so she could make sure I did something sensible with it, and we've jokingly called it a bequest so often it's become a habit."

Mike's jaw dropped. "Sensible? Blowing this kind of money on a five-day trip is *sensible*?"

Caitlin remained calm, refusing to let Mike know he'd hit close to home. "A first-class transatlantic crossing on a Cunard *Queen* was something my aunt always wanted but never could afford, even though she'd grown up in a wealthy family. You see, she was left to fend for herself at an early age."

"Orphaned?" Mike asked.

Caitlin frowned. She hated that word. "Worse," she said in an uncharacteristically curt tone. "She was an only child and her mother had died, so there was just her father. At seventeen she refused to marry the man he'd picked out for her, so he disowned her. Simply kicked her out, not giving a damn how she got along." Caitlin paused, wondering why she was telling Mike these things. Yet she kept going. "Anyway, the old tyrant died two years ago at ninety-seven, apparently repenting in his last days, though he never realized that a caring word from him while he was alive would have meant more to his daughter than the small fortune he left her in his will."

"Too little, too late, no matter how much money it was," Mike murmured.

"Exactly. Aunt Penny doesn't have much use for her inheritance. She can't go very far nowadays because of her failing health. She was determined that the same thing wouldn't happen to me, and she knew I shared her luxury-liner fantasy." Caitlin took a deep breath and smiled. "So here I am, in a sense making the voyage for both of us. And yes, Mike, to our way of thinking, blowing her father's cash on this trip is *very* sensible, not to mention satisfying."

Mike understood the reasoning. He even sympathized with both Caitlin and her aunt. Yet he still felt they were unrealistic. "What happens when the trip ends?" he asked after several moments.

Caitlin lifted her shoulders in another of her breezy little shrugs as she answered, determined to offer no hint of her own concerns about where she was going, where her whole life was headed. "I'll hit the road on the cheap in Britain for a while, and when the cash flow gets tight, I'll probably find a pub to play barmaid in for a while, or maybe sign on with another temporary office-help agency. My father was born in London, so I have no problem about work permits."

As the waiter arrived to clear the table for the next course, Mike studied Caitlin in troubled silence. Her inheritance money was gone. Within days her ocean voyage would be just a memory, and her next plan was to scrape for a living in a foreign country. The woman was hopelessly naive, and so was her aunt. Worse, he thought with a twist of anxiety, Caitlin was a loner. Something deep within him rebelled against the idea of this fragile, beautiful woman slinging beer to a bunch of tough customers in a pub, probably living in some walk-up flat in a questionable neighborhood, perhaps even hitchhiking from one place to the next.

A simmering fear gripped him. Caitlin had a deplorable sense of direction. And her kind of trust was scary. Couldn't she see the pitfalls waiting for her? The dangers? She needed someone to take her in hand and teach her a few of life's unpleasant realities. "I was talking about the more distant future, Caitlin," he said, making an effort to speak very calmly. "Wouldn't it have been wiser to make some kind of investment with your aunt's money? And couldn't the time and energy you spend tearing around and taking just any job be better used to further some serious goal?"

He was just like Pam, Caitlin thought. He had a way of hitting too close to uncomfortable truths. Yet she didn't agree with him. Didn't want to, at any rate. "The only investment portfolio I'm interested in is a nest egg of precious memories," she said tightly. If the man was determined to see her as an irresponsible fool, fine. Maybe he was right, maybe not. She didn't give a damn one way or the other. "And my single goal," she added, "is that two decades from now I'll be able to look back and honestly say I've lived twenty years, not one year twenty times."

Mike stared into her clear green eyes in utter amazement. She not only lacked direction, she didn't care where she ended up. She really didn't care. "Are you serious?" he asked at last, his personal feelings nudged aside by professional interest.

"Not if I can help it," Caitlin shot back.

"Good Lord," Mike murmured.

"You see? Shocked and appalled," Caitlin said, determined to sound as if Mike's reaction didn't bother her. And she didn't know why it should; no one else's opinion gave her any sleepless nights. "You can't say I didn't warn you," she added lightly.

Their main courses arrived, and while they were being served, Mike had time to realize the impression he'd given Caitlin. As soon as the maddeningly attentive waiter had finished spooning the sauces and arranging vegetables on their plates, Mike smiled and nodded him away, then turned to Caitlin. "Don't misunderstand. All right, perhaps I'm shocked and appalled because I'm afraid you're heading for disaster. But another part of me is fascinated. I feel like an anthropologist who's stumbled onto the missing link."

Raising one brow, Caitlin gave him a saccharine smile and deftly sliced into her steak. "Why, Dr. Harris, you do have a way with words. What brought on this latest bit of sweet talk? Have I been walking on my knuckles again?"

Mike stared at her for a moment, then groaned. "Wasn't I supposed to be proving to you that I can be reasonably sane and charming? Caitlin, I didn't mean that remark the way it sounded. It's just that I've never met anyone like you. Most of the people I encounter and associate with—patients, friends, family—are driven types, ambitious to a fault, compulsive controllers steering themselves toward shattered marriages, broken health, and an early grave. At the clinics, particularly the one in Manhattan, we try to help people change those destructive habits, so naturally I'm intrigued by someone who seems free of them to begin with."

"Has anyone ever suggested," Caitlin said in

measured syllables, deciding to let Mike take the heat for a while, "that the physician could stand to heal himself?" She braced herself for a vehement denial, perhaps even an explosion.

He fooled her. He burst out laughing. "My secretary made and framed a needlepoint sampler of that expression and put it up in my office. My partner has threatened to slip a sedative into my morning coffee. But there's a plus to sharing my patients' problems. They know I understand what makes them tick. Now, to get back to the main point, Caitlin, if you're as carefree as you suggest, you're unique."

"I didn't say I was carefree," she reminded him. "Just that there are certain worries I refuse to bother with."

"How do your parents deal with your free spirit?"

After a brief hesitation Caitlin lifted her shoulders in another cavalier shrug, this one not so convincing. "My folks took off in a small plane for a fishing trip when I was thirteen, and never came back." She realized that it sounded as if she'd been abandoned, but the proper words, the words that described what had happened, were too horrible. She'd never been able to say them. Not since the day she'd been called out of class by the neighbor she'd been slated to stay with for the week. She'd listened to the news in stunned silence, the agony so terrible, so all-consuming, she hadn't been able to cry until months later. Her young, beautiful parents had decided at last to take a holiday, a second honeymoon after years of a nose-to-the-grindstone existence building up a law practice, a partnership they'd decided on when they'd fallen in love as students at Oxford. They'd never even reached their cozy cabin in the woods. "There was a crash," Caitlin managed after a moment. "So Aunt Penny is my only family. She's in her seventies, and until her arthritis started to get really bad a couple of years ago, she'd have made me look like a timid stay-at-home—except, of course, for the half-decade of putting her own life on hold to stay with me in my boring hometown in Wisconsin. She felt I needed the stability of the same school and the house where I'd grown up. The cabin fever she must have felt was totally unnecessary. It was awful staying in that town. I died a little every time I went past the building where the law office had been, the parks where we'd gone for picnics. . . . It seemed like a mockery to have everything that mattered in my life obliterated, while the inconsequential details went on as if nothing were wrong." Caitlin stopped abruptly, horrified by her outburst. Even Pam had never got that kind of confession from her. Swallowing a lump in her throat, she marshaled all her forces to lighten up. "Anyway, I think I can safely say my aunt thoroughly approves of my so-called free spirit." For some reason Mike's opinion mattered to Caitlin more than she wanted it to, and she couldn't help adding, "I might point out that I managed to put myself through college before I turned into a happy wanderer. Now, isn't that wonderfully practical?"

A lot of things about Caitlin suddenly clicked into place for Mike. Barely hearing her last comment, he saw her as a little girl on the brink of adolescence, her whole world all at once turned inside out, her security and comfort assured one moment, erased the next. He wondered who'd had to tell her what had happened, whether the news had been broken gently or bluntly, how she'd reacted. Only a great-aunt had been available to take over as her parent; just how alone had Caitlin been during the first awful hours? Had anyone held her?

When he realized that he wanted to hold her now, to get to that little girl who still lived inside the cool young woman across from him, he found himself speaking with a false, superficial gruffness. "So for you and Aunt Penny it's a matter of grabbing all the excitement you can before the parade passes by," he murmured.

"Exactly," Caitlin said. "Perhaps someone should needlepoint that one for your office, Dr. Harris. Along with a nice little biblical quotation. 'Consider the lilies of the field' has a nice ring to it."

Mike was sorry he'd aroused her chippiness, yet he liked it. And he realized that Caitlin Grant wasn't interested in his pity, even in his sympathy. "How about something less lofty? 'Freedom's just another word for nothing left to lose' seems pretty apt," he said gently. "I think I'm beginning to understand what makes Caitlin run. She's rootless, she's basically pessimistic under the pose of a cockeyed optimist, and she's scared."

Caitlin narrowed her eyes. Damn him. Damn him for knowing. "Let's go back to calling me a free spirit. It's just as meaningless as those other words, but it doesn't have the negative overtones."

Mike watched emerald flames flaring in Caitlin's green eyes and wondered just how afraid she was of growing attached to any place or person. "Why so prickly, Caitlin?" he asked, watching her attack her steak.

She pushed a chunk of meat around on her plate, and finally put down her knife and fork. "I'm full," she announced.

Mike shook his head and sighed. "Once again, you've hardly touched your meal. And once again, you and I are at odds. Why does this keep happening?"

"Because," Caitlin said as calmly as she could, "I still say 'tom-*ay*-to' and you're a closet 'tom-*ah*-to' person."

Aware that Caitlin was barely resisting the temptation to get up and march out of the room, Mike grinned, hoping to defuse the tense moment. "Even so," he said quietly, reaching across the table to take her hand in his, "Let's *not* call the whole thing off."

As heat seemed to emanate from Mike's strong fingers into her body and his eyes at once caressed and teased her, Caitlin found herself relenting, her defenses melting. Finally, dragging her gaze from Mike's to glance at her plate, she murmured, "Maybe I'm not full after all. Maybe I'll try to eat a bit more." She looked at Mike again and managed a laugh. "I'll start with a po-*tah*-to."

Five

The ship took its first noticeable roll just as Caitlin and Mike were walking into the Grand Lounge to watch the stage show that was scheduled to start within a few minutes.

"Oh my," Caitlin said with a grin as she felt the slight swaying under her feet. "I've been hoping we'd get a bit of action. Up to now the ocean's been so placid, it's hard to remember we're at sea."

Mike smiled vaguely, musing that he was at sea in more ways than he liked. "The prediction was that we'd be going through a storm. Apparently, our resident weatherman is more accurate than his landlubber colleagues on television."

"Great," said Caitlin, beaming. "I hope things get really lively."

"Perhaps a shipwreck would satisfy your craving for adventure," Mike drawled as he guided Caitlin toward a small table with a decent view of the stage. "You're not worried about being seasick?"

Settling into her chair, Caitlin laughed. "I've been caught by squalls on the Great Lakes in a small sailboat, and I've made November crossings on the English Channel. I doubt that a little cradle-rock or two on a ship like this one will bother me."

Mike smiled. "Well, if you do find yourself getting queasy, don't suffer. Go to the infirmary for a shot."

"*Now* I'm queasy," Caitlin said, shuddering. "In the first place I would never find the infirmary, and in the second place . . . well, isn't a shot rather drastic? It seems to me there are pills that do the job. Not that I expect to need anything."

"Afraid of needles, little girl?" Mike teased.

Another flash fire blazed in Caitlin's eyes. "Afraid of nothing, big boy."

Tipping back his head, Mike laughed heartily. "You know, I'm beginning to think this voyage could turn out to be a tonic instead of a time-waster after all. And I have a feeling that you're better for me than a dozen needlepoint samplers. For some reason, when I'm with you, I don't give a thought to clinics or lectures or five-year plans."

"Five-year plans?" Caitlin repeated, carefully ignoring the flutter of excitement his words aroused deep inside her. "You chart your clinic's growth in five-year projections?"

"I chart my *life* in five-year projections," said Mike, fully aware that Caitlin would find the idea ridiculous.

She laughed and shook her head. "What happens if your life doesn't conform to the plan?"

"I don't know. I haven't had to deal with that situation. So far everything has proceeded according to schedule." Almost everything, Mike added silently. His plan hadn't allowed for a green-eyed sea witch to enchant him.

Caitlin's amusement dissolved as Mike's gaze

settled on hers and held it far too long and intensely for comfort.

"Caitlin?" she heard a very Bristish voice say.

Although it sounded far away, it broke the spell. She turned and saw an older woman at the next table smiling at her. "Oh, hi, Daphne," she said, not sure whether she was disappointed by the interruption or grateful for it. "Where's Charles?"

The woman's eyebrows shot up in surprise. "My goodness, you have a good memory." She turned to Mike. "My husband and I were just two of many people who spoke to Caitlin after she did such a marvelous job in the fashion show. You must have been so proud of her, Mr. . . . ."

"Mike," he supplied. "Mike Harris. And yes," he added with a sidelong glance at Caitlin, "I'm very proud of her."

"Mike Harris," the woman repeated thoughtfully. "You don't mean *the* Mike Harris? *Dr.* Harris, the ship's guest lecturer? The author of that wonderful book about personality types and disease?"

Mike grinned with obvious pleasure. "Since you've called it a wonderful book, I'll plead guilty."

Caitlin's forehead creased in a frown.

"That book has been a great help to my husband," Daphne said. "Charles would be the first to admit you described him in the section about people who need to control everything and everyone around them. Since he's already had a minor heart attack, he's doing his best to relax the reins a little, not to mention finally paying attention to his diet. I've tried to get him to be sensible for years, but it's you Charles has listened to."

Controlling everything and everyone around him, Caitlin repeated silently. It was, she suspected, a perfect description of Mike. She was surprised that he was a lecturer on the ship and had written a book. Usually, she encouraged people to talk about themselves, drawing them out until they were wondering aloud what was making them tell her things they'd never told anyone else. Yet she hadn't learned even the superficial details about Mike. She'd been too busy spilling her own soul. But he could have told her, couldn't he? "You didn't mention being something of a celebrity," she said, favoring him with a frosty smile.

"You didn't ask," he answered matter-of-factly. "Besides, I'm listed in the ship's program guides, so I assumed you knew. But I should have realized you wouldn't have read the newsletters that are slipped under your door at night. It would smack too much of planning your day."

Surrendering to a childish urge, Caitlin stuck out her tongue at him, annoyed that he was right.

"Oh dear," Daphne murmured. "I seem to have caused a bit of a tiff. I do apologize."

"There's no need," Caitlin said quickly. "Mike and I are just teasing." She gave him a meaningful smile. "Right, Michael?"

He couldn't help laughing. "Right, Kate," he said with a wink, then grinned at Daphne and began chatting with her, needing a moment to back off from the constantly off-center communication he shared with Caitlin, the sense of imbalance that had nothing to do with the gradually increasing undulations of the ship.

For years he'd made a point of choosing his feminine companions with great care, gravitating toward women whose ambitions equaled his own, whose priorities were much like his, whose ideas harmonized with his on most subjects—who, above all, wouldn't give him any trouble. His caution had made him a contented man, free of the hassles he saw all around him. He liked to think of himself as an enlightened male.

Except with Caitlin Grant.

The free spirit whose ultimate response when she was stuck for a better answer was to stick out her tongue had got to him.

And all of a sudden he was faced with a situation he didn't know how to control.

The ship was swaying rhythmically by the time the Grand Lounge show had ended, and a patter of rain against the windows lining the room took care of any ideas Mike might have had about another walk on deck with Caitlin.

It was just as well, he told himself as they got to their feet. If he were alone with the woman for even a moment, he just might succumb to the temptation to kiss the smooth, satiny curve of her bare shoulder.

In fact, he knew that the best way to keep himself from getting too involved with Caitlin was to make sure he was *never* alone with her. He could enjoy her company, even get a kick out of the stimulation she offered, all the while knowing there would be a natural ending to the innocent flirtation—as long as he didn't allow any opportunities to arise where he could forget himself again.

The plan seemed to work well as he and Caitlin checked out the action in the various lounges, ending up in the casino. They had a good time, laughed a great deal, and managed to keep the undercurrent of physical attraction between them from surfacing too often.

Caitlin spied an empty spot at a blackjack table and headed for it. "I think I'll try my luck here," she said as she slid onto the high stool. "How about you, Mike?"

He shook his head. "I'll watch. Gambling's not my thing."

"Why doesn't that surprise me?" Caitlin said with a teasing grin over her shoulder as Mike took his place behind her. Reaching into her handbag, she took out the hundred-dollar bill that was her gambling budget for the whole trip.

Mike was horrified as she exchanged the entire hundred for chips, but he bit his tongue. The woman obviously needed a keeper, but he wasn't applying for the job.

Caitlin placed one of the chips in front of her to indicate that she wanted to be included on the next deal. "I'll start small and see how it goes," she said, well aware of Mike's glower even though he was standing behind her.

Caitlin had played several hands—and to Mike's amazement had won all of them—when he saw a plump, grandmotherly woman leave the one-armed bandit that had robbed her. She'd spotted Caitlin and was making a beeline for her. She leaned over the bare shoulder that was driving Mike crazy. "Now, you won't forget about me tomorrow, will you?" she asked as the dealer delivered Caitlin's hand.

"Not a chance, Sarah," Caitlin said, checking her cards, then crooking her index finger to ask for another. "Eleven o'clock in my cabin." Almost absently, she made a slicing motion with her hand parallel to the table, and the dealer went on to the next person.

Sarah put her arm around Caitlin's shoulders and gave her a little hug. "I can't wait. Imagine someone like me getting fashion and makeup tips from a real live model."

Caitlin laughed, watching idly as the last player

at the table broke and the dealer proceeded to turn up her own cards.

"How lovely, dear," Sarah said a moment later. "You've won."

After Sarah had moved on, Mike gave Caitlin a quizzical look. "Unlike you, I *did* read the ship's program notes, and there's nothing in them about Caitlin Grant giving makeup lessons. . . ." He glanced at the chips she'd won and grinned. "Or about her being a cardsharp."

"The makeup lessons aren't an official activity," Caitlin said as the dealer set out another round of cards. "After the fashion show I happened to get chatting with some of the ladies in the audience." Keeping an eye on the dealer's progress around the table, Caitlin was about to go on again about the youth cult that made perfectly attractive sixty-year-olds feel washed up because they didn't look thirty, but she decided it wasn't the time or place to climb back up on that particular soapbox. "Sarah wants to look extra special for tomorrow night because she and her husband will be celebrating their anniversary," she said instead. "One thing led to another, and the upshot is that I'm going to play image consultant to her and a couple of her friends."

"Won't they expect you to perform the miracle of making them look like you?" Mike asked. "And can a young woman help with problems she won't be dealing with for a long time?"

"Ladies of a certain age are usually smart enough not to be interested in looking like me or anyone else but their own best selves," Caitlin answered. "And yes, I think I can help them. I've done a lot of it."

Mike was newly intrigued. "How did you get involved in working with older women?"

"It started with Aunt Penny and her friends,"

Caitlin explained. "Then I began giving classes at a St. Pete's social club—I'm not sure how that came about, really. Anyway, nowadays it just seems to happen. I guess I send out friendly vibrations to my elders because I genuinely like their company. Life may or may not begin at forty, but great storytelling seems to. So does a wonderful sense of humor. And in case you're deciding that I'm subconsciously seeking my lost parents, or that I'm more comfortable with the older generation because I was raised by my great-aunt, please be advised that my best friend, Pamela, has said it all before and I've agreed with her, and I still adore people who have more past than future."

Mike smiled, beginning to see that there was much, much more to Caitlin than spellbinding eyes, legs that went from here to eternity, and a restless spirit. "You know, you should be relaxing on this trip," he remarked, "but thanks to the way you've scattered your forces, you have to grab every opportunity to earn a little spare cash."

Caitlin rolled her eyes. "I don't do it for money. I do it as a favor. And because I enjoy it."

"A favor?" Mike repeated, liking her all the more yet wanting to shake her for being so impractical. "That's even worse. Your expertise is marketable; you shouldn't give it away." He brushed aside the thought of all the times the same words had been tossed at him, especially when he spent a lot of time at the storefront medical offices he and Dave had set up in poor neighborhoods with some of the profits from their rich uptown clinics. But his situation was different, he told himself. He made good money and had assured himself and his parents a comfortable future; he could afford to give a little. "Judging by the hefty collection of diamonds Sarah was sporting," he muttered, "she could pay hand-somely for tips from a professional."

"I wouldn't charge Sarah for a little session of dabbling in makeup pots," Caitlin protested as the dealer reached her. Deciding to go for one more card, she crooked her finger, saw the right card turn up, then made her usual slicing motion. "I wouldn't dream of it," she went on to Mike. "It'd spoil the fun."

For some reason her attitude made Mike see red despite his increasing admiration for her. "Caitlin, does everything have to be fun for you? Is fun all that matters?"

Caitlin lifted her bare shoulder in a tiny shrug, as if to say she wouldn't dignify his question with an answer.

And as if to tantalize him, Mike thought, though he was certain she hadn't really drawn his attention to her shoulder deliberately. She seemed unaware of her allure. "You do that a lot, Caitlin," he remarked as he struggled against the surges of desire she'd triggered in him.

"I do what a lot? Have fun?"

"That too. But I meant the shrug. You shrug a lot."

Caitlin tilted her head to one side, grinned, and began gathering up her chips. "How dreadful," she said with mock horror. "I shrug! And in public! They ought to lock me up and throw away the key."

"Maybe you ought to consider shrugging less often," Mike muttered. "You might get rich."

She smiled. "Maybe you ought to consider shrugging *more* often, Doctor. You might get happy. And don't worry too much about me and my finances." She slid off her stool, opened her purse, and poured a cascade of poker chips into it. "While you were nattering at me, I was busy racking up a quick two hundred dollars."

Mike stared at her. "But you hardly paid attention to what you were doing! How could you win that way? Or was it just luck again?"

"A combination of luck and knowing the odds," Caitlin answered. "On one of my nongoal-oriented working stints I was a dealer in Tahoe. Now, *that* experience was *really* fun." She leaned forward to kiss Mike's cheek. "I believe I'll say good night now. I know my way to my cabin, so in case you're thinking of seeing me back, there's no need. Thank you for a lovely evening." She turned to leave, glad Mike had annoyed her just enough to make it possible for her to walk away from him. She was beginning to wonder if he did it on purpose. A defense mechanism, she supposed his clinic's psychiatrists—or Pam—would call it. Mike didn't want to let the wild sparks between them set him on fire any more than she wanted her self-will to go up in flames. They were two of a kind, for all their differences.

"Caitlin," Mike said, not even close to being ready to let her go, though he didn't know why.

She turned, her chin raised defiantly. But Mike's expression made her heart stop. He looked confused. And his dark eyes weren't arrogant; they were filled with a longing that seemed to go beyond the physical desire she knew he felt for her. Suddenly, she wanted to go back to him, gather him in her arms, pillow his head on her breast, and sift her fingers through his silky hair.

Her emotional drawbridges went up immediately. Adding tenderness to desire wasn't a smart way to fight her forbidden feelings for Mike Harris.

"Caitlin, must you go?" Mike asked after a long moment.

Stiffening her spine, Caitlin nodded. "I'd better," she answered quietly. "Aunt Penny taught me to quit while I'm ahead."

After munching on an apple and a few grapes from the fruit basket in her room, Caitlin felt she could skip breakfast in the Queen's Grill. Besides, at eight o'clock mid-Atlantic time and with a restless night behind her, she didn't feel up to sparring with Mike—or, if he didn't show up, to wondering *why* he didn't show up.

Despite the constant heaving and pitching of the ship, Caitlin curled up in an armchair and worked on the detailed journal she was keeping for her aunt to enjoy, then put down some ideas for the column the St. Pete's weekly wanted her to send back from wherever she was.

She'd decided to take an against-all-odds angle on beauty tips, a series of pieces about overcoming the special beauty problems travelers encountered, but as she glanced around her spacious room with its well-lighted mirrors, walk-in closet, built-in bureaus, and even a hair dryer, Caitlin realized she would have to wait until she was on the road and traveling hitchhiker class in Britain to come up with the right inspiration. For this part of her journey she lacked no amenities whatsoever.

A visit to the on-board Golden Door Spa seemed like a better topic. Even her doctor had recommended it, she thought with an unbidden smile.

As a deep shudder passed through the ship and another roll almost upended Caitlin's basket of flowers, she decided that trying to negotiate an exercise bike or an aerobic dance class during the storm might not be the best of ideas.

It occurred to Caitlin that she should vacate her

room for a while so it could be cleaned, so she took a quick shower, did a fast makeup and hairdo job, put on a white polo shirt, tucked it into khaki walking shorts, grabbed one of the paperback best-sellers she'd brought along, and headed for . . . She smiled. She wasn't sure where she was headed. And it didn't matter. Whatever lounge she came to first would do nicely. One of the pleasures of having no specific plans, she mentally told Mike Harris with a surge of defiance, was that you didn't get lost. Wherever you decided to flop down was your destination. That was how she'd ended up in St. Pete's. She'd gone there when winter in Minneapolis—her previous stop—had gone on too long, and she'd liked it well enough to stay. And if Mike considered her kind of life weird, what did she care?

Stop thinking about that man! she ordered herself. Stop arguing with him, including when he's not around! It had been bad enough to carry on these internal debates with herself for the past several months. Adding Mike's two cents' worth wasn't helping.

Sinking into a tan leather armchair in the Queen's Room, Caitlin willed herself to concentrate on her novel. But even a thriller couldn't hold her attention; she kept glancing at passersby, and the feeble excuse that she was people-watching didn't wash. There was only one person she was watching for, much as she hated to admit it.

What was worse, her gaze kept drifting toward the dance floor as she remembered the intensely erotic moments there with Mike the night before. Her treacherous body softened at the very thought of Mike's arms holding her, his lips brushing against her skin, his deep voice and outrageous words sending shivers through her.

Read the book, she ordered herself.

She'd managed to force her attention back to her novel often enough to get through the first chapter when her new friend Daphne wandered by, saw her, and stopped. "Good morning," Daphne said in a shaky voice, perching on the arm of the chair opposite Caitlin's.

"Good morning," Caitlin returned cheerfully, then noticed that Daphne looked a little rough around the edges. "Did you have a late night?" she asked with a sympathetic smile.

Daphne groaned. "I had a terrible night. All that lurching and tossing about—I've discovered I'm no sailor. But you look fresh as a daisy, Caitlin. Hasn't the storm bothered you at all?"

"Actually, I've been finding it kind of fun," Caitlin answered. "But I don't suppose you need to hear that. How about your husband? Is he feeling out of sorts?"

"That beast is just fine," Daphne grumbled. "I've just come from the infirmary. I haven't been truly ill yet, so I took a shot to be on the safe side. Since I'm told it will make me drowsy, I have every hope of sleeping out the storm." She shook her head and sighed. "What I'd give to have an iron constitution like yours."

Caitlin shrugged. "I guess I'm lucky," she said, then realized that Mike was right. She did shrug a lot. She did seem to explain away a number of things by saying she was lucky. And the word *fun* did figure largely in her vocabulary. Was she shallow? Or scared to be serious about anything?

She wasn't too impressed by the options.

"Where's your young man this morning?" Daphne asked. "I'm awfully glad his lecture isn't until tomorrow. I should hate to miss it."

"He's not my young man," Caitlin said automatically. "We just met."

Daphne shot her a quizzical smile. "Really? How odd. I'd have sworn you two were . . ." She stopped. "Well, I must be on my way. I'm starting to feel distinctly green, and the color doesn't go well with my outfit."

Caitlin smiled and wished Daphne better health, but sat fretting when she was alone again. What had the woman been about to say? *I'd have sworn you two were . . .* Were what? Caitlin wanted to know. Lovers?

Snapping her book shut, she decided she'd done enough reading. It was becoming difficult anyway as the storm worsened, making her stomach feel a bit unsettled from the occasionally dancing lines on the page.

Gripped by a strange restlessness, Caitlin wandered about the ship, spending some time in the shops, accidentally stumbling upon the theater, and taking in a few minutes of a dull lecture on investment tactics for the nineties, finally returning to her cabin to prepare for her eleven o'clock beauty-tip lesson.

She perked up when Sarah and three other ladies arrived, all of them with their own makeup kits in hand as Caitlin had suggested. She always enjoyed the challenge of bolstering a woman's shaky self-confidence, partly by showing her a bit of cosmetic sleight-of-hand but mainly by stressing the beauty she already possessed.

"The wonderful thing is," Sarah said after she'd tried putting on her blusher the way Caitlin suggested, "I don't feel like a clown. I had a makeover once, and as soon as I got home, I scrubbed it all off. The look was fine for a young girl, but too harsh for me."

So there, Mike, Caitlin said silently. I know my stuff.

Sarah's friend Maggie smiled as Caitlin fluffed

up her silver-streaked black hair, taking away the
rigid look of the set and creating a softer frame
for her face. "What I like is that you haven't made
me feel as if everything I've been doing is wrong,"
Maggie said to Caitlin. "I'm not sitting here wondering
if I've been running around looking like a
frump without realizing it."

Caitlin laughed. "I don't have to make you feel
that way, Maggie. I'm not trying to sell you
anything."

By noon Caitlin's spirits had risen enough that
she felt up to braving the Queen's Grill for lunch,
and she'd convinced herself she didn't care
whether or not Mike would be there.

But as she reached the restaurant entrance,
her heart started thudding almost audibly, her
legs began quivering, and her insides twisted into
a knot. Only her pride kept her from retreating.

Derek greeted her with his usual pleasantries
and led her to her table. It was empty.

She'd gone into a ridiculous tizzy for nothing!

Ralph Rush looked up from the neighboring
table as Caitlin settled into her chair. "Hiya, Kate.
What happened to the doc? Is he seasick?"

Serve him right if he was, Caitlin thought. "Perhaps
Mike decided to go for the buffet," she said
aloud, picking up her menu.

A moment later she was sorry for her unkind
impulse. Nobody deserved to have seasickness
wished on him, Mike least of all. What had he
done to deserve her hostility, except to be much
too attractive? Even when he was at his most
overbearing, he had the best of motives. And was
it his fault that she let other people's outspoken
disapproval of her lifestyle roll off her while a
mere lift of Mike's eyebrow raised her hackles?

When she looked up and saw him striding purposefully
toward the table, not bothered in the

least by the constant swaying of the ship, his lithe masculinity underscored by a taupe cotton sports jacket worn over a white open-necked shirt and black slacks, Caitlin's body betrayed her all over again. The menu trembled in her hands, her skin felt hot with a sudden flush, and the smile she gave him was too bright—especially considering the way he was glowering.

"Are you going to start in on me about not eating breakfast?" Caitlin heard herself blurt out as soon as he'd sat down. "I did eat," she added lamely. "I had fruit."

"What you did or did not eat for breakfast is none of my business," Mike responded. He had put in a rotten, sleepless night, unable to stop thinking about Caitlin Grant, wanting her as he'd never wanted any woman. When she hadn't shown up for breakfast, his acute disappointment had left him no doubt about just how badly she'd shaken him up. Then, when he'd tried to take refuge in work, the real trouble had started. "If I don't seem too happy, it's because we're in a dead zone."

Caitlin blinked. "A dead zone?" She ventured a smile. "Have you been reading too much Stephen King?"

Mike didn't see any humor in her remark. "A dead zone at sea means you can't send or receive phone calls."

"Why would you want to?" Caitlin asked, instinctively reaching out to steady her glass of water as a particularly strong roll started to tip it. "Part of the charm of an ocean voyage is being more or less out of touch, isn't it?"

"I'm a doctor, Caitlin. My patients depend on me."

Caitlin realized how thoughtless her remark

had been. "Of course, Mike. I'm sorry I was so cavalier about the situation."

Relenting instantly, Mike realized he was using the dead zone as an excuse for what really was bothering him. After all, the radio officer had told him that a cable was possible in the event of an emergency. And other doctors had been assigned to his patients. "No, Caitlin, *I'm* sorry," he said with a sudden smile. "I snapped at you as if it's your fault that we're out of phone contact. The truth is, if I can't check in with the clinic, I won't have to listen to my partner giving me a hard time about not being able to delegate responsibility for even a few days."

"You really do have a lot of trouble letting go, don't you?" Caitlin said gently. "And yet you've chosen that very tendency to zero in on as a health hazard."

Mike grinned and deftly caught the salt shaker as a heave to starboard sent it sliding off the edge of the table. "As I said to you once, I understand the problem. I can identify with others who suffer from it. But now to more important matters: First on the agenda, let me say that you look terrific, as always." He tried not to think about the fact that she wasn't wearing a bra under her knit shirt. "Second, let's order lunch. Then I'd like to hear all about your session with Sarah and company."

"You would?" Caitlin said with unmasked surprise.

"I would. For all our differences you and I do seem to have one thing in common: We both have an affinity for our elders. I'm concerned with bashing the myths and changing the health habits of a society that still believes aging has to mean a diminished quality of life, and I gather you're trying to do the same thing in your way."

He skimmed through the menu selections with forced casualness, hoping his unquenchable desire for the woman across from him didn't show. "What are you going to have?" he asked as he felt her gaze resting steadily on him.

Caitlin had to rouse herself to answer. She was in a slight state of shock, not sure she'd heard right. Had Mike compared her mascara-and-blusher efforts with his obvious dedication? "Oh . . . I thought perhaps I'd go for the chilled cucumber soup to start," she said absently, "then I guess I'll try the cold lobster salad . . ." She took a deep breath, all at once feeling rather strange.

"Sounds good," Mike murmured. "I think I'll order the salmon terrine as my appetizer and the seafood linguini for a main course. It'll probably be rich, but what the hell, it's still fish. And anyway," he added with a self-mocking chuckle, "it's time I lived dangerously." He snapped the menu shut and smiled at Caitlin, determined to have an enjoyable lunch with her and just forget all the adolescent urges raging through him. Surely, he was adult enough to control them.

His smile faded abruptly. Caitlin was staring at him as if he'd turned into one of Stephen King's most horrifying specters, her eyes huge and startled, her complexion drained of color.

In the next instant she was on her feet and racing from the room.

Six

The instant Caitlin walked out of the washroom, she spied Mike. "Go away," she said miserably.

He smiled and slid one arm around her waist while pressing the call button for the elevator. "Time for a seasickness shot, I'm afraid. I'll take you to the infirmary—in your present state I don't think you'd manage to find it."

"I'm not seasick, and I don't want you to miss your lunch on my account."

"I'll get a sandwich from room service," Mike said reasonably. "And you most definitely are seasick."

"Quit saying that!" Caitlin groaned. "My stomach's a little upset because . . ." She stopped abruptly, realizing she didn't want to tell Mike he had caused the original butterflies that had got a little out of control.

"Because?" Mike prompted. The elevator arrived, and he guided Caitlin onto it.

"I want to go to my cabin," Caitlin said as Mike pushed the button for Six Deck. She wished her voice would sound less shaky. She wished her whole body would *feel* less shaky. "If you're trying to take me down to the infirmary, forget it," she said, reaching past him to push the One button.

"Caitlin, you're being silly," Mike scolded.

"Fine. I'm being silly. But I don't happen to think I'm seasick, so I don't intend to take a shot. Anyway, I wasn't . . ." She paused to gulp some air as her surroundings began spinning again and a cold shiver passed through her body. "I wasn't all that sick," she managed to say in a strangled voice.

Mike couldn't believe her stubbornness. "Caitlin, for Pete's sake . . ."

"I won't go to the infirmary, and you can't make me!" she snapped, then winced at the childishness of her outburst. "I mean, you're not really my doctor. And I was fine until I went to the Queen's Grill." She shut her mouth, realizing she was on the verge again of confessing that Mike himself had given her a nervous stomach.

"The rolling of the ship is more pronounced up here," Mike said as the elevator door slid open at One Deck. "You're seasick, Caitlin. The sooner you admit it and give in to having a shot, the sooner you'll feel fine again."

Relieved to step from the tiny cubicle that had added to her queasiness, Caitlin started walking briskly to her cabin. "I'll compromise. My cabin stewardess said she has seasickness tablets. I'll take one. But I'm not seasick."

Shaking his head, Mike followed her, caught her by the upper arm, and drew her to a forced halt.

Caitlin gave him the fiercest look she could summon. "Mike Harris, don't you dare try to   "

"Honey, you're headed in the wrong direction," he interrupted with a grin that changed to a frown an instant later. He wasn't in the habit of using endearments like *honey.* "Your cabin's the other way," he added gruffly, once again sliding his arm around Caitlin's waist.

Suffused with sudden warmth, Caitlin told herself that the waves of heat from Mike's touch had nothing to do with the rise in her temperature. Probably, she had a touch of the flu. A fever. That was it. Clammy one minute, burning up the next. It had to be fever.

When they reached her cabin, Caitlin pulled the key from her pocket and tried to fit it into the lock. Trembling, she was feeling too ill to be anything but grateful when Mike took the key and opened the door. "Since you're being so obstinate, I'll give you a pill," he said, reaching into his pocket and pulling out a small white envelope as he shut the door.

Caitlin sank onto the edge of the bed and stared up at him. "You have some with you?"

"It's seasickness weather. Of course I have some with me." He picked up a glass and went to the refrigerator he'd noticed in the walk-in closet. "Good. You have mineral water." He opened the bottle and filled the glass. "You know, Caitlin, I don't understand why you won't admit what's wrong with you," he went on as he returned to her. "There's no shame attached to being seasick. It can happen to anybody—including me. Seasoned sailors have told me that there's a particular rhythm out there for everyone; the one today just happened to have your name on it."

Caitlin accepted the pill and the glass of water he handed her. "Are you always prepared? For anything and everything?" she asked between swallows.

Not by a long shot, Mike answered silently. He hadn't been prepared for Caitlin Grant or for her effects on him. "I do my best," he muttered. "Now get into bed."

Caitlin glared at him and would have made a comment about the way he barked out orders, but a great roll of the ship made her think better of trying to say anything. She slipped her feet out of her sandals and curled up on top of the covers.

"*Into* bed," Mike said with an exaggerated sigh of impatience. He couldn't believe what was happening inside him, the burning coals of desire that not even Caitlin's gray-green hue and the beads of cold sweat on her forehead could douse. "Caitlin, at least take off those shorts and get under the blanket. You'll feel better."

Caitlin groaned. Mike was right. Her waistband was actually hurting her stomach, and she was shivering from the cold. But she had her pride. And her modesty. Mike wasn't just a doctor, and when she was with him—even feeling sick—she couldn't think of herself as his patient. Their relationship was charged with extremely unprofessional undercurrents. "I'll get undressed as soon as you leave," she said at last.

"I'm not leaving," Mike informed her. "So get undressed now. I'll go to the washroom to get a cool cloth ready to soothe your pretty, fevered brow, but if you're not out of those shorts and under the blankets when I come back, I'll take care of the matter myself."

"All right, all right," Caitlin interrupted. "Lord, you're a bossy son-of-a—"

"Be nice, Caitlin," Mike said calmly as he headed for the washroom. "Profanity doesn't become you."

While he was gone, Caitlin's mutterings were unbecoming, but she forced herself to get up and take off her shorts, deciding her polo shirt and bikini panties made fine pajamas.

She was in bed when he returned, her eyes

closed, and the blankets drawn up under her chin.

Another rush of primitive need overwhelmed Mike; with his knees threatening to buckle, he was glad for the excuse to sit on the edge of the bed. Using one corner of the cloth he'd prepared, he stroked away the perspiration from Caitlin's forehead, battling the crazy urge to climb into bed and simply hold her. He'd never felt that way before about any woman.

He placed the cool compress on Caitlin's forehead. "You'll be drowsy soon," he said as soothingly as he could, though his throat was constricted and his voice sounded thick. "And the ship's movements aren't as pronounced on this deck."

"I'm not seasick," Caitlin mumbled.

Mike shook his head and smiled as he got to his feet.

Caitlin opened her eyes. "Are you leaving?"

"I thought I'd stick around to keep an eye on you," he said.

"You don't have to do that," Caitlin said. "You've already been more than kind, and I haven't been very gracious about it all."

Impulsively reaching down to trail his fingertips over Caitlin's cheek, Mike said quietly, "Wouldn't you like me to stay for a little while?"

Caitlin hated to admit she didn't want him to go, and she didn't feel she had the right to accept his offer, but she closed her eyes and nodded almost imperceptibly.

Mike stood gazing down at her for a long moment, refusing to examine the reason for the surge of joy that seemed to be making his heart swell in his chest. "I'll get some room-service sandwiches and tea delivered," he said in a voice that had gone husky. "Maybe you'll feel like nibbling on something later."

"I wouldn't count on it," Caitlin murmured, disturbed by the weakness that had made her ask him to stay.

As Mike picked up the phone and put in his order, his glance fell on a notebook lying on the bureau. He saw the title printed in a neat hand: *QE2 Diary: For the Ladies of a Certain Age.*

After he had hung up, he went to the washroom and prepared a fresh cloth for Caitlin's forehead. "So you're keeping a diary of this voyage?" he asked as he returned to her. Sitting on the bed again, he removed the old compress and replaced it with the new one.

Caitlin made a sound that Mike took as a yes.

"Is it private?"

"I don't think so," she mumbled. "It's for Aunt Penny and some of her friends."

"Do the people you're writing for mind being referred to as 'ladies of a certain age'?"

"That's the name I've given them," Caitlin said, managing a tiny laugh. "*They* call themselves 'old broads.' "

"Mind if I read it?"

Caitlin thought for a moment. She'd mentioned Mike in the journal, but not by name. And she hadn't included her most private thoughts and feelings about him. "Go ahead," she said at last. "But you might find it dull. Full of details. I'm trying to make my aunt and her friends feel as if they're along on the trip. I think I'll leave out this part, though. Who needs it? I feel awful."

"What a thoughtful gesture," Mike said, amazed by the sheer volume of Caitlin's efforts as he riffled through the pages. "This is quite a project."

Caitlin gave a tiny shrug that Mike could see through the covers. "It's the least I can do." She paused to make sure a small wave of nausea wasn't getting the best of her, then went on hesitantly, "My . . . my aunt is giving me something she can't have because . . . because of her failing health." Another pause, then a deep breath, then Caitlin continued, "Instead of being envious of me, Aunt Penny and her friends looked forward to my trip as much as I did. I want to share it with them."

On an impulse Mike bent down and kissed each of Caitlin's closed eyelids. "You know, you're very sweet."

Startled and touched by the gesture, Caitlin opened her eyes and gazed at Mike as he straightened up. When the tenderness of his expression threatened to shatter her few remaining defenses, she said, "You mean besides being obstinate and irresponsible and naive and skinny . . ."

"You're not skinny," Mike objected, finding his pulse accelerating as he was drawn into the bottomless depths of Caitlin's soft green eyes.

Caitlin wondered how she could be so sick and yet experience the wild urges that were coursing through her. Didn't her body have any sense at all? "Not skinny, then," she said, clinging to her shreds of resistance. "Just obstinate and irresponsible and naive."

"And sweet," Mike reminded her, taking the compress and smoothing it over her temples, her cheeks, and her throat while he stroked her hair with his other hand.

All at once something happened inside Caitlin; she hoped it was the pill's effects clicking in. Otherwise she had no explanation for the sudden softness pervading her, the strange sense of release, the unprecedented letting go of tensions she hadn't been aware of on a conscious level, even though she knew they'd been part of her for years. She grew extremely drowsy. "You're kind of sweet yourself, Doc," she murmured, adding after a moment, "for a bully."

She went to sleep to the sound of Mike's quiet laughter.

Mike sat watching her for a while, wishing Caitlin would stop arousing his tenderness. Tenderness meant trouble.

Leave, he ordered himself. She's fine. She doesn't need you now.

But he couldn't force himself out of the cabin, so he took off his jacket and settled into an armchair with Caitlin's journal.

He was astonished by the wealth of detail she had included in her descriptions of every aspect of the voyage, by the way she'd recreated the sounds, the aromas, the flavors, the textures of life aboard the *QE2*. Several passengers and crew members came alive with a turn of phrase that was rich with affectionate humor. Even Ralph Rush was oddly appealing, and there was gentle empathy for Bunny's doomed struggles to remain a sex kitten forever.

The more he read, the more he was struck by the strange sense that Caitlin was doing more than trying to share her voyage with the ladies of her aunt's circle; she almost seemed to be taking it more for their sake than her own, garnering experiences denied to them.

She should have titled it *The Substitute Traveler*, he thought, glancing over at her, watching her sleep, wondering about her in countless ways.

He read on until he came across a tall, dark, handsome stranger, spoken of lightly as a perfect touch for the fantasy of an adventure on the high seas. She'd spotted him for the first time on the pier, in the next lineup. . . .

Leaning his head against the back of the chair,

Mike closed his eyes and allowed himself to remember every moment with Caitlin, to daydream about how things might be if he weren't so infernally cautious. . . .

When Caitlin woke up, the storm was at what she hoped was its height, buffeting the ship like a winter wind against a hilltop cabin.

Her glance flitted about the room, then stopped suddenly. She blinked. Mike hadn't left even after she'd gone to sleep. Why not?

He was sitting in his shirtsleeves in the armchair across the room with his feet on the coffee table and her journal lying open against his chest. He was sound asleep.

She propped herself up on one elbow and studied him for several moments, amazed by how vulnerable he looked, how boyish and unguarded.

She found herself wondering what made him tick, why he seemed so driven, whether he ever wanted to let life just happen instead of trying to stage-manage it as if it were a play. Perhaps it was true that she was bumbling along without goals or direction, but wasn't it just as foolish to keep to a narrow path that didn't allow for any surprises?

It occurred to her that the room was slightly chilly; she remembered that there was an extra blanket in the closet.

Getting out of bed, she was pleased to find that she was steady on her feet again, not the least bit seasick.

She took a moment to slip into the washroom to freshen up, including a vigorous tooth-brushing and liberal lacing of mouthwash, and immediately felt even better. After remembering to put everything away in the medicine cabinet where it would be safe despite the movements of the ship, she went to the closet, pulled the blanket from the overhead shelf, and tiptoed back to Mike.

Carefully taking the journal out of his hands and placing it on the coffee table, then tucking the blanket around him, Caitlin gave a start when his fingers suddenly curled around her wrist.

"I'm sorry," she whispered, straightening up. "I thought you might be cold. I didn't mean to wake you."

He stared up at her with an intensity that robbed her legs of their strength. "I was dreaming about you," he said after a long moment. "About us."

Caitlin couldn't say a word. Her heart was pounding wildly, the throbbing beats echoing in her ears as her blood raced out of control. Mike's gaze slid downward to her breasts, and she realized they were swelling with a surge of desire, their tips hardening and thrusting against the thin cotton knit of her shirt. When he slowly continued his perusal, she felt as if he were passing a white-hot flame close to her body, and as he reached out with his free hand to touch her thigh, she felt the heat as if it were a brand.

With her wrist remaining locked gently but firmly in his grip, he met and held her gaze again, gliding his free hand over the long, sweeping curve of her thigh. "Are you feeling better?" he asked just above a whisper.

Caitlin nodded, still incapable of speech, her faculties overwhelmed by wave after wave of desire.

"I should leave," Mike said, making no move to go. His fingers tightened around her waist. "I don't think I can fight this battle anymore," he said very quietly. "Not unless you want me to fight it. Tell me to leave, Caitlin. Just say the words and I'll go."

Swallowing hard, Caitlin remained silent.

She shuddered as his fingers slid under her hip-length polo shirt and touched the wisp of satin beneath. After tracing its lacy edges, he feathered downward to the back of her knee, discovering a spot there that she hadn't realized was erotically sensitive.

"You're so beautiful, Caitlin," Mike murmured, sitting up straight and pushing aside the blanket. He released her wrist and began a new journey as his palms slid upward over her hips, moving under her shirt to skim over her waist and midriff, finally caressing the tender underside of breasts, the whole time imprisoning her with his eyes while she supported herself with her hands on his shoulders.

She wondered vaguely if she had been mesmerized into compliance. Why hadn't she taken the opportunity he'd given her to put a stop to something she was certain to regret? Why was she submitting to Mike's bold exploration?

Alive to his touch, her body leapt as his fingers brushed over and around her nipples. "Take off the shirt, Caitlin," Mike said, his tone quiet but sure, as if he expected her to do his bidding without question.

She tried to rebel, but her limbs were becoming heavy, breathing was becoming a chore, and she wanted to be free of the constraints of clothing. She liked Mike's hands on her, liked their warmth and strength, ached to feel them on every inch of her flesh. Curling her fingers around the hem of the shirt, she stripped it off and tossed it aside.

Mike's scrutiny of her almost-nude body was like the concentration of the sun's rays through a shard of glass lying on dry leaves, building an intense, smoldering heat that could burst into an open conflagration at any moment. Sliding his arms around her, he drew her closer and slowly brushed his lips over her taut stomach just above the scalloped edge of the bit of lace that was her only remaining claim to modesty.

With a sharp intake of breath, Caitlin tipped back her head, her back arching as Mike retraced his trail with the tip of his tongue. "I knew you'd be delicious," he said, his breath warm against her skin. "I knew from the first moment that you'd taste of . . ." He drew his tongue over the inside of her hipbone as if sampling her to verify the evidence of his senses. "Of cinnamon and vanilla," he said at last, hooking his fingers under her elastic lace waistband and tugging downward just a little, tracing another horizontal line of kisses and hot, teasing licks of his tongue across her belly. With excruciating patience he drew the panties down, savoring her at his leisure until she was gasping with pleasure and heightened need.

Mike felt as if he were back in his dreamworld as Caitlin finally stepped out of her single tiny garment and stood totally naked before him, responsive to his every touch, her fingers twining through his hair as he covered her torso and thighs with kisses and let his hands roam freely over her body, gently kneading the perfect mounds of her breasts, stroking her long, slender back, and at last venturing to explore the most intimate secrets of her femininity.

Finally, when she was flushed and moist and eager for him, Mike got to his feet and gathered her close, holding her with one arm while he began undoing his shirt. He savored her full lips, nibbling and stroking until her tongue was meeting his in a loving ritual dance.

When his shirt was undone, Caitlin pushed it

apart and slid her hand over his chest, her fingers splayed as she fluttered them through the coils of chest hair and brushed them over his hard male nipples. She was caught in a vortex of passion and a driving need such as she'd never known before. She wanted Mike. Wanted him to ease the ache and fill the emptiness within her.

Yet she felt the rise of a familiar panic. If Mike did ease that ache, did fill that emptiness, what then? Would they be lovers until Southampton, then cheerfully wave good-bye and go on with their separate lives as planned? Could she bear that loss?

Mike instantly recognized the sudden tension in Caitlin. He summoned every ounce of willpower at his command, grabbed the blanket, and wrapped it around her. "You're right," he said tightly, wishing she weren't trembling so violently. He felt rotten. "What the hell did I think I was doing?" he said, pulling her hard against him.

Caitlin tipped back her head to stare at him. "I didn't say a word!"

"You didn't have to, Caitlin. When you remembered all the reasons why we have no business doing this, I could sense it in your body. And it's true. We have no business doing this. I had no business . . ."

An awful thought struck Caitlin for the first time. "Good grief, are you involved with someone else? Have I wandered onto some other woman's property?" As soon as she'd spoken, she knew she'd chosen her words badly.

Mike curved his hands around her shoulders and set her away from him. "Hear this, Caitlin Grant. I have never been and will never be any woman's *property*."

"I didn't mean it that way, Mike. . . ."

"Moreover," he continued. "I never have been and hope I never will be a cheat. When I make a commitment to someone, I won't play around with anybody else."

Caitlin felt terribly bleak. Who would be that special to Mike? Why did it hurt so much to know she couldn't be the someone who would have his love and loyalty?

Determined not to let him suspect her feelings, she drew the blanket closer around her and smiled. "Well, let's not get too heavy about all this. Fortunately, we stopped before we went too far. I suppose I should thank you."

"You'd have more to thank me for if I'd been decent enough not to take advantage of your vulnerability. I'm sorry, Caitlin. Whether or not you believe me, I didn't stay here for that reason."

"Why did you stay?" she asked in a small voice.

Mike wasn't sure how to answer. It would sound crazy to admit he'd stayed simply because he hadn't been able to make himself leave. "I . . . I started reading your journal. It's wonderful. I see why that newspaper editor in St. Pete's is happy to get your columns. You're a talented lady." He studied her for a long moment, then shook his head. "You could do anything you liked, be a success beyond most people's wildest dreams. I wonder why you don't." Without waiting for an answer, he pressed a kiss to her forehead. "Have another nap. I'll come by around eight and see how you're doing. If you feel up to the Queen's Grill, we'll go have dinner."

Caitlin narrowed her eyes and marched over to the bed, holding her blanket around her as she flopped down on it theatrically and curled up as if to go right to sleep. "Yes, sir. One nap coming right up, sir," she muttered.

Mike shook his head and laughed as he headed

for the door, though his insides were tightening painfully at the tempting vision of Caitlin in bed. He ached to crawl in beside her and pull her to him spoon style, to feel her back against his chest, the curve of her bottom nestling perfectly into his loins, her breasts high and firm and eager for his caresses. "I'll see you at eight," he said in a suddenly hoarse voice, adding on an impulse he didn't understand. "And tonight we're going to have a long talk about your plans for England—or perhaps I should say the plans you *don't* have for England."

Caitlin's lower lip thrust out in a pout. "I'll be just fine tonight, but you don't have to come to pick me up," she called out to him as he opened the door to leave. "I can find my way to the Queen's Grill on my own these days. And I fail to see why we need to have a talk about my plans *or* the lack thereof for roaming around Britain."

Mike laughed again, and was gone.

Caitlin cursed herself. He hadn't responded. She had no idea whether to expect him at eight or not.

She spent the rest of the afternoon trying to convince herself she didn't care.

Seven

Mike knocked on Caitlin's door at precisely eight o'clock. He was calm. Pulse normal. Blood pressure fine.

Then Caitlin opened the door.

An ankle-length tube of clinging, stop-sign-red jersey skimmed over her body from a low-cut halter neckline, and Mike's heart screeched to a halt as he stared at her. After a timeless moment the beat picked up slowly, heavily, erratically, accelerating until it was pounding with an uneven throb that seemed to echo along the corridor.

He cleared his throat. "At the risk of sounding British before we even get to Southampton," he said with an effort, "you look smashing."

Caitlin responded with a tiny, wary smile but didn't meet Mike's gaze as she stepped out into the hall and turned to lock the door, wondering if he *had* to look so devastating in his tux. "I wasn't sure you'd pick me up," she admitted.

"Why not? I said I would."

"But I told you not to bother."

Mike had recovered his poise enough to grin.

"When did I give you the impression I'd jump to your command?"

Dropping her key into her handbag, Caitlin said in a too-sweet drawl, "Oh, that's right. I keep forgetting. You're the one who *gives* orders."

"Now you're getting the idea," Mike retorted as they started down the hall. His tone was jocular, but he was as uneasy as Caitlin. Noting that she still wasn't meeting his gaze, he decided to deal with their awkwardness head-on. "You're feeling fragile," he said quietly, putting his hand on the small of her back as they reached the elevators.

"I'm fine," she answered too quickly. "Your pill worked wonders."

"I wasn't referring to your seasickness."

"I wasn't seasick."

"Okay, let's say you had *mal de mer.* Does that sound more acceptable? But I meant that you seem nervous. Even shy." Mike pushed the call button to summon the elevator.

"Why should I be shy?" Caitlin said, trying in vain to sound offhand. "We passed *shy* somewhere south of Iceland."

The elevator arrived and they stepped on; Mike was glad they had it to themselves. Obviously, there were some barriers to be dismantled before they reached the Queen's Grill. "Let me put it this way," he said as the doors slid shut. "The balance of power is tilted too far in my direction."

Caitlin suddenly found the beadwork on her evening bag utterly fascinating.

Mike spanned her waist with his hands, turning her to face him and drawing her closer. "It's a question of control, Caitlin. You surrendered it this afternoon for a while; I started that session we had, and then I stopped. Unless I miss my guess, you're angry with yourself for all of it. And you're just skittish and unreasonable enough to have decided I was toying with you."

"Weren't you?" she said in a small voice, still staring at her bag. "Didn't you get what you wanted? Wasn't the fun over once you knew you could do whatever you liked with me?"

Mike's first impulse was to be angry. This was his thanks for trying to be a gentleman? For showing a few scruples? His second urge was to ask Caitlin just where she'd got her suspicious ideas about males.

But his third impulse was the one he acted on. "I won't pretend not to have enjoyed knowing I could do whatever I liked with you," he said carefully. "And your response gave me—though I hesitate to admit it—a sense of power that still has me half-intoxicated. I'm tempted to push the 'stop' button on this elevator to stall us between decks, peel that terrific red number right off your delectable body, and savor every inch of you all over again." As he watched a flush stealing over Caitlin's throat, saw her nipples harden and strain against the thin jersey of her dress, and heard the immediate raggedness of her breathing, he crooked his finger under her chin and made her look up at him. Her eyes were dark and glazed with rekindled desire. "Oh yes, Caitlin, I revel in the effect I have on you," he said in a soft, caressing tone. "But it was the woman I wanted this afternoon, not just that rush of pleasure." He gathered her closer and murmured against her ear, "And if you don't know that you affect me just as powerfully, that you could turn the tables on me and tip the scales your way any time you chose, you're far more innocent than a grown-up lady like you ought to be."

The elevator doors whooshed open, and Mike

released her before Caitlin could say a word. It was just as well. She'd lost the power of speech.

They entered the long, narrow cocktail area outside the Queen's Grill. Like the restaurant, the lounge was decorated with clean lines, soothing colors, and the kind of art-deco accents that underscored Caitlin's impression of a thirties Astaire film. With one wall completely given to windows, it was a perfect place to sit and contemplate the ocean.

Mike noticed Caitlin's glance going to the white leather tub chairs by the windows. "Would you care for a drink before we go in for dinner?" he asked.

Caitlin was tempted, but sea-watching didn't strike her as a wise activity at the moment. She fluttered her eyelashes at Mike in mock helplessness. "You mean I'm allowed a drink?"

"A soda wouldn't do any harm," he said pleasantly. "And if you're trying to bait me about being domineering, don't waste your time. I've recognized the tendency, and I'm working on it."

Caught off guard by his frank admission, Caitlin couldn't help laughing. "Working on it? You could've fooled me, Generalissimo."

"Don't judge by the way I am with you," Mike said with a grin. "You bring out the dictator in me. Now, do you want to stop for a drink, or should we go right to the dining room?"

"I'm going to the dining room," Caitlin said without hesitation. "I'm starved. But if you want a drink first, don't think you have to escort me—"

"Don't be silly," Mike cut in, cupping his hand under her elbow.

To her annoyance, Mike's flat refusal to let her go ahead without him warmed Caitlin as much as his touch. But she continued to wrap herself in lightheartedness, as if it were a cloak that could shield her from dangerous emotions. "Why do I bring out the dictator in you?" she asked, managing to sound casual.

"I'm not sure. I think it's because I get the feeling you need one." They reached the dining-room entrance, and Mike pushed open the glass door, nodding to the maître d'. Derek's greeting to both of them was jovial enough to take the sizzle out of any retort Caitlin was planning.

On the way to their table Mike noticed how many people spoke to Caitlin as though she was dear to them—all of them old enough to be not just her parents but her grandparents. Mike admired the special rapport she had with seniors; he assumed it was another result of having been raised from adolescence by her great-aunt, and he was beginning to understand why Caitlin seemed to belong to another era, despite her up-to-the-minute stylishness.

Just after they were seated, the wine steward arrived. "I don't think we'll want anything this evening, Jason," said Mike, deciding it wouldn't be fair for him to have wine with dinner when Caitlin shouldn't.

Caitlin looked up from her menu. "Now you're the one who's being silly. Believe it or not, I can watch you drink wine without feeling compelled to grab the bottle and slug back a belt myself."

Mike looked at Jason, and they exchanged who-can-argue-with-a-woman smiles. "I guess we do want something this evening," he said. "The usual, then."

Jason nodded, his eyes twinkling but his cool aplomb not slipping a bit. "The Château Millet, sir. Very good."

"There now, Caitlin. You see?" Mike said after Jason had left. "I'm not so bossy after all. You made me change my mind with hardly any effort."

"And suppose I'd tried to order wine for myself?"

Mike smiled. "In all conscience I'd have had to discourage you. We aren't sure whether you really are over your seasickness, and the waters are still pretty rough."

"I wasn't seasick," Caitlin said patiently, though she was becoming a little weary of this broken record. "What I am is ravenous. I'm going to start with caviar, move on to the chilled raspberry soup, then devour the chicken stuffed with foie gras and truffles. . . ." She shut the menu and smiled. "I'll decide about dessert later. Believe me, this is one time when you won't be able to accuse me of picking at my meal."

"Naturally. This is the one time when you *should* pick at it. Instead, you're going to assault your stomach with the richest food you can find. Do you work at being hard on yourself, Caitlin?"

"Do you ever stop being a preachy doctor, Doctor?"

He held up one hand in a warding-off gesture. "Truce, okay? For the rest of the evening I'll bite my tongue whenever I'm tempted to launch into a lecture. And I was going to start in on you about the vagueness of your plans for England, but I'll back off. Fair enough?"

Caitlin was wary. "Almost too fair. Are you up to something?"

"Just trying to make sure I see plenty of that beautiful smile of yours," Mike answered quietly.

She had to struggle to keep her lips from turning upward at the corners, and as Mike's heated gaze softened her brittle facade, she barely noticed their waiter's arrival. "Caitlin?" Mike said, politely indicating for her to order.

She looked up and hesitated. Knowing that Mike was right about her menu choices, she considered changing to a more sensible meal. But she wasn't in the mood for the consommé, broiled chicken, and plain steamed vegetables she ought to have. Besides, she'd let Mike have the upper hand long enough; it was time she put her foot down. "I'll start with the caviar, then . . ."

Mike made no further comment about her foolishness, and by the end of the meal he thought perhaps he'd been wrong. Caitlin seemed to be thriving, unperturbed by a constant rolling motion of the ship that was strong enough at moments to make a couple of quick catches necessary to keep the wine bottle from taking flight. Even when Ralph Rush and his Bunny stopped to chat on the way to their table, Caitlin was bright and charming and friendly.

Caitlin herself was pleased with the evening so far. The truce was working; she and Mike were having fun, sharing anecdotes and exchanging lighthearted bits of their life stories and even teasing each other in a good-natured way about their diametrically opposed personalities and outlooks.

But she did start wondering halfway through dessert whether having pistachio ice cream with hot fudge sauce might have been a little excessive. She was beginning to feel warning flutters in the pit of her stomach. Pride kept her from showing her discomfort as she tried to ignore the rhythmic weaving of the ship, though at one point she felt as if she were perched precariously on a high stool in the middle of an undulating waterbed.

"Coffee?" the waiter asked.

Caitlin shook her head. "I'm trying to kick the habit." She leveled a meaningful look at Mike, who was on his second cup. "I hear it's bad for you," she added, then realized that her pride was about to be betrayed by a stronger force. "Would you excuse me, Mike?" she said, making a great effort to smile and speak calmly.

She got to her feet and kept her head high as she headed for the door, but as soon as she was out of the dining room, her pace quickened, and by the time she'd reached the familiar washroom by the elevators, she'd broken into a dead run.

When she emerged ten minutes later, Mike was waiting. "It seems to me we've played this scene before," he drawled.

Caitlin glowered at him. "If you say you told me so, I swear I'll arrange to have you thrown overboard."

"I don't have to say I told you so," Mike replied with forced cheer, pressing the call button for the elevator. "You already know it. And now it's time for your shot."

"I'm not going for a shot."

Mike raised his brow and gave her a sharp look. Was there something wrong with her that he didn't know about? Was he interfering where he shouldn't? "Do you still insist you're not—"

"All right!" Caitlin interrupted. "I'm seasick!"

Mike rolled his eyes. *Now* she was admitting it, just when he wasn't sure what to think. The woman was impossible.

Caitlin added in a small but determined voice, "But I don't need a shot."

"You need a shot," Mike said grimly.

The elevator arrived, and the doors slid open. There was another couple inside.

Knowing Mike's planned destination, Caitlin hung back. "It's too crowded in there," she protested.

He simply put his arm around her and started forward, and Caitlin couldn't retreat without making a scene.

Mike pushed the button for the dreaded Six Deck.

Caitlin made a try for One, but Mike smiled and hugged her closer, somehow pinioning her arms at her sides.

When the elevator stopped on the next deck down, the other couple got off, and Caitlin tried to go with them.

Mike tightened his arm around her.

On Six, he urged her on. She tried to stay on the elevator. "You go ahead," she told him in a last-ditch attempt to avoid the inevitable. "I'll catch up with you."

He laughed and shook his head.

A moment later Caitlin found herself entering the infirmary's waiting room. Two people were there ahead of her. They looked like refugees from Mars.

Caitlin's stomach lurched. "I'll take a pill," she whispered. "Two pills. But I don't need a shot."

"You really are scared of a little thing like a needle," Mike said in a low voice. "Miss Afraid-of-Nothing will let her entire dream trip be ruined because she can't take a tiny jab that lasts just an instant. Funny, I hadn't figured you for a chicken."

Caitlin glared at him. "I'm not a chicken. Where do they stick it, anyway?"

"What? The needle?"

"No, the chicken. Of *course* the needle!" she said, almost forgetting to keep her voice down.

Mike scowled. "In the usual place. Why?"

"What usual place?" Caitlin demanded. "The arm?"

"That's not the usual place I mean," Mike said, struggling to suppress his grin as a strangled groan escaped Caitlin. "What's this? Are you modest as well as scared?"

"I'm neither. I just don't care for . . ." She sniffed. "For the indignity of it all. Who gives the shot, anyway? A nurse, maybe?"

"You'll like the ship's doctor," Mike assured her. "I met him when I was given a tour of the onboard medical facilities. He's a fatherly type."

"I hate fatherly types," Caitlin grumbled. It wasn't true. She would take a gentle fatherly type ahead of a young Captain Bligh any day.

She paled as an inner door of the infirmary opened and a nurse beckoned to one of the Martians, leaving a single person between Caitlin and the dreaded hypodermic. She'd die before admitting it to Mike, but needles terrified her.

Mike favored her with an innocent smile. "Would you prefer to have your own doctor do the honors? I promise to be gentle, Caitlin. Back at the clinic, everybody asks for Dr. Harris when it's time for a shot."

Caitlin's eyes widened. "Not on your life, Mike Harris! You are *not* my doctor!" Glancing at the other patient, an older woman whose eyes had widened at the last remark, Caitlin smiled feebly, plunked herself down on a straight-backed chair, and folded her hands in her lap like a prim schoolgirl, pressing her knees together and looking directly ahead. "I'm starting to feel better. It's stupid to get a shot. Seasickness isn't in my genes. You can bet that Aunt Penny never had to have a shot when she crossed the Atlantic, and she sailed on horrible old ships that got tossed about like paper sailboats, not on luxury liners like this one."

Mike shot Caitlin a quizzical frown. Was Aunt Penny the reason for this nonsense too? Was Caitlin trying to live up to an impossible image?

A few minutes later the one remaining patient was entering the doctor's office. Caitlin's number was almost up. Deciding to make one more escape bid, she darted a glance at Mike as he lowered himself onto a chair beside her. "You were right," she conceded grudgingly, though for her own purposes. "It's the exaggerated motion of the ship on the higher deck that gets to me. Nothing more. I don't need a shot. I'm fine now." She started to stand up.

"So all you have to do is spend the rest of the voyage here in the infirmary, and you'll be in great shape," Mike said as he caught her arm and pulled her back to a sitting position, effectively ending the discussion.

They sat silently until the petite but curvaceous nurse came out, gently escorted her trembling patient to the door, then looked up and saw Mike. "Why, Dr. Harris," she said, her big brown eyes lighting up like a Broadway marquee, "how lovely to see you again. But surely *you're* not seasick?" She let her glance flicker slowly over him and said in an unmistakably suggestive tone, "You look healthy enough to me."

Caitlin's eyes narrowed, and she could almost feel her fingernails extending like claws. "I'm the patient," she said with a smile that was more like baring her teeth. "My doctor was kind enough to accompany me here." She emphasized the *my* just a little.

Mike barely managed not to chortle out loud. "That's right," he said, reaching out to take Caitlin's hand and gently pulling her up from her chair. He was taken aback by how cold and tense she was, and suddenly the whole situation didn't strike him as quite so amusing. He wondered why she was so frightened of a minor, ordinary moment of discomfort. "My patient," he said, duplicating Caitlin's particular emphasis, "is just a little shaky on her sea legs."

The nurse didn't even glance at Caitlin. "Does she need a pill?" The woman's expression as she gazed at Mike was nothing short of worshipful.

"She needs a shot," Caitlin snapped, pulling her hand away from Mike's and striding into the office.

Staying back for a moment, the nurse winked at Mike. "One of the nervous ones, right, Doctor?"

Mike smiled and nodded absently, startled by the acute surge of protectiveness racing through him. He felt as if he were abandoning Caitlin to a terrifying fate; his professional detachment was history.

When the nurse finally left him and joined Caitlin, closing the office door, Mike realized that for the first time since he'd become a doctor, he truly understood the emotions of the expectant fathers he'd seen pacing outside delivery rooms; of the hand-wringing parents who had to stay in a reception area while their children were given stitches; of every relative or friend who had waited for news of a loved one from an emergency ward.

On his personal scale of stressful situations, he decided, this one ranked near the top. And not far from it was the tension he felt as he puzzled over his pleasure in Caitlin's obvious burst of jealousy.

His reaction was totally perplexing. Mike didn't like jealousy in women. The slightest display of it was guaranteed to send him packing. Yet he was buzzing inside with a strange excitement because Caitlin's green eyes had flared with angry possessiveness.

He assumed a nonchalant manner when Caitlin came out, her face flushed and her bottom lip swollen where she'd been chewing nervously on it. "Did you get it over with?" he asked with a sympathetic smile.

She nodded, clutching her small handbag with both hands, as if it could steady her.

Mike thanked the nurse and put his arm around Caitlin's shoulders to lead her back to the elevators and her cabin.

She was subdued, not even giving him the satisfaction of an argument when he went with her into her room and ordered her to bed. She undressed in the washroom, emerging wrapped in a fuzzy pink robe, and Mike's arms ached to enfold her. "I'll get you some water," he said with difficulty, disappearing long enough for her to crawl under the covers.

When he returned, she was lying on her back, staring at the ceiling. Placing the water on the nightstand, he sat on the edge of the bed and gently touched her cheek. "You're not having much fun on this dream trip of yours," he murmured.

"Neither are you, thanks to me," she said, her lip quivering a little.

Mike smiled. "But for me it wasn't meant as a dream trip. I have to be in London on Friday to speak at a medical convention, and I'd have flown except that I was asked to be a lecturer on this voyage. Even then I'd have refused, but Dave—David Masterson, my partner—aroused my curiosity about demographics. It seems the typical *QE2* passenger is a lot like our average clinic patient in terms of age and income bracket. Dave pointed out that I could plug my book to a crowd that was likely to be interested, have some sort of vacation, and at the same time do some research by observing these people at play. He insisted that it was of great value to know whether the workaholic rich really relax on a five-day ocean voyage or just find another outlet for their nervous energies."

"The way you do," Caitlin couldn't help pointing out.

Mike chuckled quietly. "Which brings me to the main reason Dave took it upon himself to arrange for my passage on this ship: He wanted me out of his hair. I wouldn't be surprised if he bribed the elements of nature to put us into the dead zone I told you about."

Caitlin found herself smiling a little. "Are you really that much of a pain?"

"So I gather," Mike said. "I don't mean to be. But I do have trouble taking vacations, and I can't seem to help sticking my nose into all aspects of the clinics, and as you already know, I always think I'm right about everything."

"In my case your opinion has been justified," Caitlin said ruefully. She heaved a deep sigh. "I did some thinking while I was in the doctor's office. It struck me that you didn't have to be the least bit concerned about whether or not I took a shot. You didn't have to take me by the hand to make sure I did the sensible thing. You didn't have to . . ." She swallowed hard. "You haven't had to do any of the thoughtful things you've done since I met you." She searched his eyes for a long moment. "Why, Mike? I flippantly asked you this once before, but now I'm really wondering: You could have any woman you wanted. Why are you bothering with someone as difficult and ungrateful as I am?"

Mike smiled and traced the outline of her mouth with the tip of his index finger. "Who knows? You get to me, that's all. I have no other explanation." Realizing that once again he wanted to take Caitlin in his arms and simply hold her, that he longed to lie beside her and cuddle her for the whole night without even hoping to ease the pent-up frustration inside him, that he cared about her in a way that made no sense in the larger picture of his existence, he sighed and shook his head. "You just get to me," he said softly, then bent to kiss her forehead. "I'd better go now. That shot will put you to sleep soon. And it'll work, Caitlin. Tomorrow morning you'll be yourself again, no matter what the seas are like."

Caitlin managed a smile, though she felt sudden tears stinging her eyelids. Ridiculous, she thought. Why should she be so moved by Mike's tenderness? Why should his words touch a deep, secret part of her that she'd never allowed to surface? Why should she wish fervently that he would climb into bed beside her and surround her with his warmth?

And why, she asked herself immediately, would the man want to do a dumb thing like that?

" 'Night," she said as he got to his feet and started for the door.

" 'Night," he answered.

He was opening the door when Caitlin heard herself calling his name.

Mike stopped in his tracks, then turned and slowly went back to stand at the foot of the bed. Was she going to ask him to stay? Was he out of his mind to hope so?

Caitlin gazed at him for a long moment. "I didn't thank you," she said at last.

Despite his disappointment, Mike smiled. "The pleasure was all mine, honey. Now go to sleep."

The room seemed terribly empty when he was gone.

Caitlin was grateful when the shot's effects set in, and she felt the drowsiness pulling at her. She didn't want to face the feelings that she couldn't deny much longer.

Eight

Caitlin opened one eye as she heard the knock on her cabin door, then sat up, fully awake, when the door opened.

"Sorry to disturb you, mum," the cabin stewardess said in her Scottish lilt, breezing into the room bearing a tray. "Your doctor asked me to deliver your breakfast. He was very choosy about it, too, I must say. What's more, he says if you don't eat it, I'm to report your wickedness to him directly. Where would you like it, mum? Right there in bed?"

"On the coffee table would be fine," Caitlin murmured, rubbing the sleep from her eyes. "I'll get up." She considered sending the tray back to the kitchen just to make the point that she didn't take orders from Dr. Michael Harris, but she was hungry, and the fruit cup was tempting. There was plain yogurt on the side, with a small jar of honey for sweetening. And it seemed that Mike had allowed her a croissant, even a pot of tea. Her beleaguered stomach leapt with eagerness. "Thanks very much, Maggie," she said to the stewardess. "You needn't worry; I'll eat every morsel. I'm starved. What's the weather like this morning?"

"Still a bit rough, but the worst is over," Maggie said cheerfully. "Shall I open these curtains, mum? There's no sunshine yet, but a bit of light might cheer things up."

"That'd be lovely, thanks," Caitlin said, reaching for her robe and swinging her legs around to get out of bed.

"Now, don't let me down, mum," Maggie said as she bustled toward the door. "You eat every bite, or I'll have to tattle to that lovely doctor of yours."

Clamping her lips together to keep from saying that Mike was *not* her doctor, Caitlin managed a smile. "Every bit," she promised as she sat down.

Maggie hadn't closed the door behind her before Caitlin had dived into the food to keep her promise.

An hour later, fed and showered and dressed in white linen slacks, brightly striped espadrilles, and a chrome-yellow shirt nipped in at the waist by a wide white belt, Caitlin felt ready to take on the world. The shot had worked wonders, much as she hated to admit it. And it hadn't been all that bad. Thanks to Mike, perhaps she'd taken the first step toward getting over that particular phobia.

Tucking her journal into a large white bag that she'd slung over her shoulder, she left her cabin and saw Maggie coming down the corridor. "You can report that I demolished my breakfast," she told the smiling stewardess.

"That's good, mum. If you don't mind my sayin' so, I'd do the same in your shoes. When that doctor of yours says somethin', he means it in no uncertain terms."

Caitlin rolled her eyes in heartfelt agreement and set out for the Queen's Room.

She chatted with several people there, then sat down and worked on the journal, hardly aware that she was watching the clock. But a short while before eleven she stopped writing and headed for the theater, finding it after only two false starts. A respectable crowd had gathered, including most of Caitlin's newfound friends.

She was settling into her aisle seat in a middle row at the very moment when Mike walked across the stage to the podium. He immediately spied her and broke into a grin.

Caitlin sat down hard, her legs giving out. Dressed in the same gray slacks and silk-tweed blazer he'd worn on the first night of the voyage, Mike looked strikingly handsome, but it was his lopsided grin that cut through whatever shields she'd managed to put up. She gave him a shy smile in return, then hastily averted her gaze.

She noticed Daphne shooting her a knowing look, and could almost hear the woman saying again, "Mike isn't your young man? But I could have sworn . . ."

Caitlin didn't want to know what Daphne could have sworn. She was too busy swearing herself, wondering why she'd decided to take in Mike's lecture. Hadn't she spent more than enough time with the man? Didn't she have to face him for several more meals before reaching Southampton? Wasn't she getting tired enough of his lectures without seeking out an opportunity to listen to a formal one?

What really annoyed her was that she was nervous, wanting every person in the theater to agree that Michael Harris was the most wonderful doctor since Hippocrates, the most charming male since Cary Grant, the greatest orator since John F. Kennedy.

She couldn't envision it happening, considering the unpalatable truths Mike was likely to drive home to an audience composed largely of longtime smokers, success addicts, and connoisseurs of rich food and drink. An "Ask not what your body can do for you, but what you can do for your body" kind of speech wouldn't go over too well.

Mike was only a few minutes into his talk before Caitlin realized she'd underestimated his powers of both persuasion and observation.

Obviously, he hadn't been wasting any of his time during the past couple of days, she mused. He knew the members of this group as if he'd been studying them for years. He had no trouble couching his message in terms they found palatable, and they soon grasped that this doctor wasn't a cocky young whippersnapper presuming to preach to his elders, but a dedicated physician who admired them for surviving and excelling in a pressure-cooker world. He wasn't piously condemning of his listeners for their bad habits; he pointed out that many of them had grown up in an era when cigarettes were endorsed in advertising by everyone from movie stars to doctors to future presidents. He didn't shout the medical equivalent of a fire-and-brimstone diatribe against high-fat diets, sedentary lifestyles, and overwork; he suggested that all the people attending his lecture were showing their usual initiative just by being there, by being ready to take control of their own health.

His glance went to Caitlin at that point and rested there until she squirmed with self-consciousness, like a student whose professor has just leveled a criticism without mentioning any names but making sure everyone knew who the culprit was by singling her out with a steady gaze.

She could have throttled him.

Mike went on then in a relaxed, chatty manner, citing upbeat case histories and funny anecdotes to illustrate how even small changes in what he called "life management" could yield big dividends in long-term "quality control." The business terminology was calculated, Caitlin suspected. Mike was a clever man. A brilliant puppeteer, she thought with a slight start.

She also realized that most of Mike's advice could be gleaned from popular fitness magazines, yet he made the possibilities seem exciting, made simply truths sound boldly imaginative, made small sacrifices sound easy when measured against the rewards.

She was managing to become quite cynical about him until he disarmed her by saying just what she'd been thinking: that nothing in his lecture or his book was particularly revolutionary except that his familiar truths were backed nowadays by convincing scientific evidence.

The beast, Caitlin thought. Did he have to be so modest? So sincere? So infernally charming?

She wondered what her aunt would think of Mike. Probably that he was handsome and smooth and a delightful reason to indulge in some lighthearted flirting, Caitlin decided, but not the kind of man to get too involved with. Aunt Penny would spot his domineering tendencies right away, and issue stern warnings against him.

The trouble was, the imagined admonitions of her beloved aunt couldn't compete with the reality of Mike, the impact of his magnetism, even the sound of his voice as he wound up his remarks.

"All I'm suggesting, ladies and gentlemen," Mike

said at last, "is that you treat your body as well as you treat the Cadillac in your driveway. If you do, you just might be surprised by the mileage still on it."

The only vehicle Caitlin had ever owned was a secondhand bicycle, and she'd let the tires go soft and the gears seize up and eventually made it her contribution to a spring cleanup campaign, but she applauded Mike enthusiastically.

As he left the stage and began heading straight toward her, Caitlin felt singled out again, but this time in a way that made her excited and proud that he was her . . . She frowned. Her what? Certainly not her doctor, despite all the nonsense they'd both indulged in on that subject. Was he her friend? The word didn't seem adequate. Mike was something else, something more—yet she couldn't call him her lover.

He was a crush, she told herself. An infatuation. It had been bound to happen to her some time. She'd been lucky to escape that kind of foolishness as long as she had.

She saw that he was trying to reach her, but he couldn't get past the bodies that suddenly surrounded him, people wanting special attention, personal advice. "Don't leave?" he said, causing a number of heads to turn and several curious gazes to fasten on her.

It was the upward inflection at the end of his words that made Caitlin nod and stay in her seat instead of bolting, hiding from Mike Harris and the terrifying feelings he aroused in her. The plea that was in his voice in place of the usual command simply paralyzed her.

After what seemed like an endless wait, Mike finally managed to excuse himself from his enthusiastic but demanding fans by suggesting a time later in the afternoon when he would arrange to answer further questions in the Queen's Room. Then he made his way to Caitlin. "Hi," he said as he held out both hands to her, investing the small word with enough warmth to melt any part of her that wasn't liquid honey already. "Do you feel as great as you look?"

She got to her feet and mustered a grin. "I just hope I look half as great as I feel—thanks to you. The shot did its job—I buzz-sawed through the breakfast you sent me, and I expect to enjoy the rest of the voyage even if the dining room *is* like a circus ride."

"Are you game to give it a try?" he asked as they left the theater.

"On one condition," Caitlin said, shooting him a sidelong glance, her grin becoming more natural. "You do the ordering."

It bothered Mike that he hated to part from Caitlin even long enough for her to go to the Golden Door Spa while he headed for the Queen's Room to field more questions about his book and his medical viewpoints. If being away from her for a few hours was difficult, how was he going to feel when he had to say good-bye to her in Southampton?

Suddenly, a memory flitted through his mind of Dave and all the rest of his clinic colleagues urging him to follow his appearance at the London convention with a genuine vacation—no lectures, no notes, no work at all.

He almost laughed. A vacation? He hadn't taken one in years. He couldn't. He had patients to think about. There was Mrs. Bannerman, for instance, his favorite octogenarian with the mid-Victorian "palpitations" in a heart as strong—but as lonely—as any he'd encountered. She'd been upset to learn that he was going to be out of the country even for a week, and since he'd been caught in a crazy dead zone, he hadn't been able to call her just to say hello and reassure her that Dr. Masterson was eager to prove he could be just as attentive and comforting as Dr. Harris. Then there was the crusty oil baron who was scared silly of what his tests might show up, and the . . .

Mike stopped. If he were his own patient, he would advise himself to do something pleasurable and absorbing to take his mind off such useless fretting.

He knew exactly which pleasurable and absorbing activity would do the job, but seducing Caitlin to provide himself with a diversion didn't strike him as very honorable. And seducing her for any other reason conjured up complications he had no room for in his life. Her seasickness the previous night had been timely, forcing him to step back and take a long, sane look at his feelings for her, and he'd decided that those emotions had to be curbed.

Unfortunately, when he'd looked down at the lecture audience in the theater and spied her, his wise decision had been erased from his mind like data on a computer screen disappearing in a power outage. All he'd known was that seeing her sent a deep thrill through him. All he'd remembered was his pulsating desire for her. All he'd cared about was finishing the lecture and getting to Caitlin, touching her, talking to her.

And he was supposed to say good-bye to the woman within forty-eight hours?

He wasn't sure he could do it.

As always, Mike was bowled over by the way Caitlin looked when he picked her up at her cabin for the last formal-dress night of the voyage.

"I don't know much about fashion, but I'd say that dress would be the ultimate little black number," he said as he took in the long slither of jersey Caitlin wore, its skirt split up the side to the thigh for a tantalizing glimpse of sheer black stocking. At first glance the dress seemed almost stark in the simplicity of its cut, the scooped neckline anchored by narrow straps at her shoulders.

Then Caitlin stepped into the hall and walked ahead of him for a moment, and Mike felt a rush of heat go through him like a flash fire: The thin straps constituted the entire back bodice of her dress, a network that criss-crossed from her shoulders to her waist and was tied there in a casual knot, inspiring visions that made Mike break out in a light sweat. He wondered how he would get through the evening without losing his resolve. His very sanity.

As they entered the Queen's Grill lounge, Caitlin smiled at Mike. "This time I would like to stop here for a drink before dinner. The ocean has settled down, and it looks as if there'll be a wonderful sunset."

"Good idea," Mike agreed, guiding her toward two empty seats beside the window, almost exactly where he'd sat brooding during the late afternoon, thinking about Caitlin and his five-year-plan approach to life and the sudden doubts he was feeling about his whole existence. His *predictable* existence. He'd watched a shaft of sunlight thrust through the gray cloud cover and dapple the sea with shimmering gold, and he'd found himself hoping for a clear night, wanting to present it to Caitlin as if it were his gift, his own doing.

"I love the ocean," Caitlin murmured as they sat quietly after the waiter had taken their orders.

"You're a forgiving woman," Mike said with a smile. "The ocean has been less than kind to you." He hesitated, then said carefully, "Are you as forgiving with people?"

Caitlin was uncomfortable with the question, sure that Mike was referring to the intimate moments that had left her feeling vulnerable and confused. "Actually, I make voodoo dolls and stick pins into them," she said lightly.

Mike winced. "I think you've just explained a mysterious pain I've been feeling in the region of my heart." He was joking, yet as soon as he'd said the words, he knew they were true.

Southampton began to seem much too close. Mike wished he could throw out a sea anchor to hold back the ship.

In an echo of his troubled thoughts Caitlin said, "It's amazing how quickly these five days are whizzing by. We're well over halfway to England already, and . . ." She paused as her throat tightened. Clearing it, she went on in a slightly constricted voice, "And we'll be having dinner together just one more time after tonight. It seems sort of . . ." Her words faded as she looked away from Mike and stared at the remarkably quiet sea.

"How long do you plan to stay in Britain?" he asked.

Caitlin started to shrug, caught herself, and slowly lowered her shoulders. "I have an open return flight from London to New York." Though she still doubted the wisdom of her plans, she smiled and spoke as if she were eager to hit the road. "First, I'm going to spend a few days with Pam—the English friend I've mentioned to you. Then I'll explore Oxford for a bit before I head out for my walk."

"A walk," Mike repeated. "You're sailing to England to go for a walk."

Caitlin sensed the seeds of another clash—and suspected she wanted one, as if she couldn't be comfortable with Mike unless they were having at least a small spat. She chose to ignore the memory of several moments when they'd been far from any kind of tiff. "I'm talking about a *long* walk," she explained. "Through the Cotswolds. And then perhaps I'll do another hike further north, in the border regions of the Sir Walter Scott stories. I might even carry on up to Scotland."

Mike absorbed that information for a moment. Then he said, "You're taking guided walking tours?"

Caitlin shook her head. "I'll be on my own."

"On your own as in alone?" Mike asked, his tone taking on a sharper edge.

"That's usually what it means," she answered with a lift of her chin.

"Dammit, Caitlin!" he exploded.

Caitlin gave a little jump, as did several other people.

Mike took a deep breath to try to calm himself, then spoke more quietly, and in carefully measured syllables. "You get lost on the *ship*, woman! How are you going to find your way around a whole bloody country?"

"Since I won't have any particular destination in mind, it won't matter if I get lost," she said with what she knew was maddening reasonableness.

"You'll end up sinking in a bog," Mike predicted, his jaw clenching and his eyes turning to steel blue as he glared at her, imagining all the disasters she was going to bring down on herself. "You'll hitch a ride with a Yorkshire strangler.

You'll wander around in circles in Sherwood Forest, and there'll be no Robin Hood to save you."

Caitlin's courage faltered just a little; she couldn't deny that she'd had nightmares about similar fates and worse, but she'd told herself she was being melodramatic. "Well, what's an adventure without a little danger?" she said in a defiant but tiny voice.

"Why?" Mike demanded, barely controlling a fury he hadn't known he was capable of. The woman had no sense at all. He'd known from the start that she needed a keeper. A keeper? She needed to be kept, all right. Under constant watch. "There are all sorts of guided tours. Why do you have to do it the hard way? The idiotic way, to be blunt?"

"And never let it be said that you were anything less than blunt with me," Caitlin said. She allowed herself only a moment to wonder about the joyous excitement surging through her. She was a placid person. Why did she love battling with Mike? Or was she after something else? Just what was she responding to when he narrowed his eyes and coiled his sleek body like an enraged mountain lion because of some scheme of hers that he considered harebrained? "I'm not quite as dumb as you seem to believe," she informed him in her best how-dare-you-insult-me manner. "I intend to follow well-used country roads, not trail off over the moors like Cathy looking for Heathcliff. And for your information, I actually did prepare for my little outing: I took courses, one in reading topographical maps and one in self-defense. I flunked the map test, but I was at the top of my judo class."

Mike wasn't placated in the least. "Great. I hope you can take down five guys before they jump you."

Caitlin burst into laughter that was only slightly tinged with nervousness; she was *not* going to succumb to her fears. "Mike, for heaven's sake," she teased, "we're talking about Jolly Olde England, the home of tea parties and good manners and fair play."

"The land of Jack the Ripper," Mike added pointedly.

Caitlin paled but chose not to respond directly to the remark. "Really, it sounds as if you'd have me be a sissy. What I'm planning is nothing! In her heyday my aunt was an adventuress in the best sense of the word. Aunt Penny rode camels in the desert, worked with missionaries in China, and did a stint as a teacher in the Australian outback. She joined the WACs during World War Two and was in the thick of combat. Surely, I can manage a stroll through England's cottage country!"

"What does Aunt Penny have to do with this discussion?" Mike said. "Or does she have everything to do with it? With everything, period?"

"What are you suggesting?" Caitlin asked, though she knew perfectly well. Pam Jennings had suggested the same thing: that Caitlin was trying too hard to live up to Aunt Penny.

"Never mind," Mike said, deciding to get back to the immediate issue. "I thought you said you were going to get a job." Compared to the plans he'd just heard, the thought of Caitlin playing barmaid in a pub didn't seem so terrible.

Caitlin was trembling inside. Mike had infuriated her in a way Pam never had, though he'd merely suggested what Pam had stated bluntly. "I said I'd get a job if I needed cash," she told him, trying her best to sound unconcerned but not quite managing it—which annoyed her to no end. "But first I want to see the countryside." She chose not to speak of her compulsion to visit the places her parents had talked about, her need to feel some remnant of their presence, their happiness. He'd think she was really crazy if she said all that. "I want to see fields and gardens and picturesque villages," she went on instead. "Up close and under natural conditions, not from behind the windows of an air-conditioned tour bus. Of course, you wouldn't understand *that* particular ambition, Mike. It doesn't lead to any profit except experience. Worse, it might involve some discomfort, like pitching a pup tent and crawling into a sleeping bag, or actually getting rained on, or feeling the full heat of the sun on a hot afternoon. Good heavens, in your antiseptic luxurious, carefully orchestrated—"

"Predictable?" Mike put in helpfully.

Caitlin quailed slightly, but squared her shoulders and barreled ahead. "Yes, predictable. In your predictable world such things can't be allowed to exist." She stopped abruptly as she saw thunderclouds building in Mike's eyes; the sky over the Atlantic at the height of the storm hadn't been half as ominous. Perhaps, she thought as she swallowed hard, she'd gone too far in goading him. And she didn't know why she'd done it. Obviously, he brought out the rebel in her, just as she supposedly aroused the dictator in him. "I'm sorry for that last crack," she said softly. "It was uncalled for."

Mike merely sipped his bourbon, not saying a word for a very long time as he lapsed into deep thought.

"Mike, I'm really sorry," Caitlin said again. "I could cut my tongue out."

He looked at her as if just remembering she was there, then focused his attention on her mouth. "Don't do anything rash," he murmured, his voice low and suggestive. "I seem to recall that it's a very nice tongue. I can think of all kinds of reasons not to cut it out."

His words were like a flaming arrow shot directly into the cache of explosives hidden deep inside her. Flares shot through her body, and fireworks burst into incendiary cascades that filled every particle of her being. "Haven't you heard of the Marquess of Queensbury Rules?" she whispered. "You don't fight fair."

Mike slowly wagged his head from side to side. "If I have to fight at all, I don't see the point in following rules, Caitlin. You'd do well to remember that."

She stared at him, trying to comprehend exactly what he was telling her. "You sound rather . . . forbidding," she murmured.

Mike smiled. He'd been told before that when he made up his mind about something he became so intense, he seemed almost threatening.

In that case, he thought, he didn't wonder at the sudden widening of Caitlin's eyes. At this moment he had to be nothing short of menacing.

Nine

For Caitlin, dinner with Mike that evening was tense and strained—and unbearably exciting.

She felt alive as never before. Hardly knowing what she'd chosen from the evening's menu, she nevertheless savored every morsel.

The Château Millet that had been Mike's choice of red wine all week and that he was pouring for her without hesitation was smooth enough to be dangerous; Caitlin made a mental note to be cautious about how much she drank. "How does it happen that I'm allowed wine tonight?" she asked after a sip that flowed over her tongue like liquid music. "Has my doctor given up trying to keep me on the straight and narrow?"

Mike smiled at her over the rim of his glass. "As you've pointed out from time to time, Caitlin, I'm not your doctor. If I were, I wouldn't have a problem with letting you have wine this evening; you've been eating properly all day, so you're not likely to get a headache or an upset stomach. But keeping you on the straight and narrow is a job that needs more commitment than a mere doctor can offer."

Caitlin put down her glass very carefully, determined not to let Mike see the sudden trembling that had gripped her. What did he mean? What was he suggesting? Fight! she ordered herself, though she was losing track of what she was fighting for. Or against. "You know, you have a tendency to be condescending," she said as she picked up her fork and speared a hapless vegetable on her plate.

"I do know," he agreed. "It goes with being domineering. As I told you, I'm working on the problem."

Caitlin's eyes narrowed. "And as I told you, Mike Harris, you could—"

"Right. I could've fooled you. But you're the cause of my backslide, Caitlin. From the beginning you've made my good intentions fly out the nearest porthole. I just get to thinking I'm not a bad guy after all, and suddenly you're on the scene, and I'm Attila the Hun."

Unexpectedly, Caitlin giggled. "The urbane Mike Harris a barbarian? I can't picture you exchanging your exquisitely tailored white dinner jacket for a few pelts, a breastplate, and a two-horned beanie. The image just doesn't work."

But a wave of heat assailed her as she found herself trying to envision what Mike looked like without either kind of clothing, and another swell followed the first with the shocking remembrance of how well he knew every inch of her body, when she had yet to see more than his bare chest.

Had yet to see, she thought, startled by the implication of her phrasing.

Forcefully, she returned her attention to her meal. Verbal sparring with Mike was a mistake; it served only to lead her along a path filled with emotional traps.

* * *

After dinner Caitlin made a halfhearted attempt to escape Mike and his unnerving spell by saying she wanted to try her luck in the casino again. To her surprise he was ready to do the same.

"You said gambling wasn't your thing," Caitlin protested.

"It wasn't," Mike answered. "But I've spent some time observing these informal research subjects of mine at play, and while I was at it, I overcame my phobia."

Caitlin was surprised again; she hadn't expected to hear Mike admit to what he would consider the weakness of a phobia. That kind of problem belonged to her, not to him. "Did you actually fear it?" she asked, her tone more gentle than it had been all evening. "Were you worried that you might discover you were compulsive or something?"

"My father used to gamble—and lose," Mike answered after a hesitation. He'd never told that bit of his background to anyone. "Dad's a dreamer, an idea man, the kind who should be paid to sit around thinking up great schemes and new ways to do things. But not many people pay for that kind of creativity, so until I . . . until Dad got some financing from somebody who had faith in him, he watched other people develop projects that should have been his."

Caitlin hadn't missed Mike's near-slip, and she had no doubt just who had believed in his father enough to finance an idea. "And when your father got his backing, did he make one of his plans work?"

Mike grinned, suddenly filled with pride. "In spades, Caitlin. And not just one idea. Several. Dad's an entrepreneur of the first order nowadays, and Mom—who always believed in him and didn't kick up a fuss even when he'd blown the household budget to smithereens—has discovered that she has the skills my father is still short on for day-to-day management. They're a team. And Dad no longer feels compelled to be drawn into a casino in the hope of making a quick hit. Unfortunately, it's taken me a while to get over the knot I used to get in my gut if I so much as saw a postcard of Reno or Vegas, or if—" Mike stopped, appalled by the extent of his confession.

Wondering if she was beginning to understand why Mike was so determined to stay in control of his life, Caitlin saw by his expression that he hadn't intended to say as much as he had. She knew he had to back off a little. "The big trouble with serious gambling," she said lightly, "is that needing to win usually guarantees that you'll lose."

Mike was taken aback, not by the observation itself but by the fact that his reckless Caitlin had made it. Yet as he recalled the way she'd handled herself at the blackjack table, he realized that she hadn't seemed reckless or particularly concerned about winning or losing. "I don't get it," he said aloud as they strolled toward the casino. "From what you've told me, you can't afford to blow a hundred dollars, yet you blithely bought all those chips and hardly paid attention to the cards."

Caitlin laughed. "You don't have to be an Einstein to add up to twenty-one; I paid enough attention to know when to stay with my cards and when to go for another one. And the hundred dollars was my entire gambling budget for the week. I was prepared to spend that much to enjoy the casino action, so if I'd lost it all, I'd have chalked it up to a good time. Winning anything is a bonus."

"Amazing," Mike murmured, giving Caitlin a quizzical smile. "You do have some sense after all." He slid his arm around her waist and gave her a quick hug. "Maybe a lot more than I realize."

"And perhaps a lot *less* sense than *I* realize," Caitlin heard herself blurting out.

They both laughed, but a look passed between them that shook Caitlin; she realized that Mike wasn't the only one who had revealed more than he'd meant to. She had allowed him a glimpse of her inner doubts. It wasn't something she did easily.

The battleground between them began to be strewn with dropped weapons as a gradual cease-fire was established.

After a few modest wins and losses Mike suggested a walk on deck. Caitlin was too eager for a breath of fresh air to refuse—and too lulled by sheer enjoyment to resist the temptation to be alone with him.

Even when he excused himself to make a brief detour before going outside, Caitlin waited in dreamy contentment, responding only vaguely when some passerby spoke to her.

"All set," Mike said as he returned to her side.

She smiled and let him lead her outside. "It's perfect," she said softly when she felt the surprising warmth of the breeze and gazed up at the low-hanging stars. "Why aren't the decks crowded? Why do people stay indoors on such a night? Why bother sailing to Europe instead of flying unless you love the sea?"

Mike smiled. "Who knows? Snob appeal, perhaps. The last of the great transatlantic superliners as status symbol. Others just want to get across the ocean, and they'd swim before they'd get into a plane. And don't forget the comfort factor. Even I'm ready to admit that air travel can't compare. What's more, there's no jet lag."

"One thing about you," Caitlin said in a tone that was gently teasing, "when you're asked a question, you don't stint on the answer."

They had reached the stairway that led to the sports deck. Laughing good-naturedly, Mike noticed with pleasure that Caitlin mounted the steps as soon as he gestured toward them. He was glad she wasn't in an argumentative mood, though he'd been prepared to harness her feistiness for his own purposes, fully aware of the simmering desire just under her surface.

He wondered if he was being cold-blooded about the seduction he was planning. He certainly didn't *feel* cold-blooded. But he was guilty of premeditation, even if he'd made his decision only a couple of hours before.

For a man who always charted the course of his life down to every possible detail and never wavered from that path, he'd done a remarkable about-face. He'd begun the evening determined to keep his feelings for Caitlin under control, at least until he was on dry land where he could get some breathing space, some perspective on what might turn out to be nothing more than the shipboard infatuation both of them kept insisting it was.

Then she'd dropped her bomb. In one casual announcement she'd rendered his plans obsolete. Within the space of a few moments he'd gone from fighting his emotions to admitting that he was incapable of leaving Caitlin to her own devices. Her misguided and inadequate devices. In fact, he was incapable of leaving Caitlin at all.

Leaning her forearms on the sports-deck railing, Caitlin breathed deeply of the salt air as she watched the aquamarine froth that bubbled up in the wake of the powerful ship. "Not a soul," she murmured. "I remember the first day, when the weather was still clear, this deck was wall-to-wall sunbathers. It's almost eerie how empty and quiet it is now."

"Didn't I tell you? I reserved this spot for us," Mike said, suddenly wishing he could have done just that.

Caitlin gave him a sidelong glance. "I wouldn't put it past you," she said, though she knew he was teasing. She turned to rest against the railing and tipped back her head to close her eyes and pretend the ship would sail forever, if only so she wouldn't have to say good-bye to Mike.

She refused to think about that parting. There was no escaping it, but she didn't have to dwell on it yet.

Suddenly, she saw a waiter appear bearing a silver tray with two tulip glasses and a bottle of Moët Chandon in a silver ice bucket.

"Well done, Alastair," Mike said with a grin.

The young man looked quite pleased with himself as he placed the tray on a table at one end of the deck near the stacked-up lounge chairs, then disappeared as silently and quickly as he had arrived.

Caitlin realized that Mike must have made arrangements when he'd left her for those few minutes before they had come out on deck. "There's something to be said for planning ahead after all," she admitted with a delighted laugh. "You know, for a pest you really are a lovely man."

Mike felt a twinge of guilt. Would Caitlin think he was a lovely man if she knew what was on his mind?

But he poured the champagne and reminded himself that she was an adult. She had to have some idea why a man would romance her so extravagantly. And she wasn't exactly unwilling.

"What's the other thing on the tray?" Caitlin asked, unable to contain her curiosity any longer as Mike handed her one of the champagne glasses.

"You'll see," he said with a wink.

An instant later she heard the lush music of her favorite era drifting across the deck. "How did you manage to supply the phantom orchestra?" she asked, utterly amazed.

"Where I go, my trusty little tape deck goes," Mike said, smiling. "How else could I be a bona fide workaholic? But where I go, my torch-song album goes too. How else could I be a frustrated romantic?"

Caitlin shook her head. "But how did Alastair get it from your room? And how did you talk him into it?"

"Suddenly, the lady who doesn't even bother to find out why she was upgraded is curious," Mike teased. "What's romance without a little mystery?"

Caitlin smiled. "How very . . . unpredictable."

Mike held out his hand to her. "And now, may I have this dance?"

She went into his arms without hesitation. They moved lazily to the music while sipping their champagne, and once again she felt her senses awakening to new awareness: the tickle of the bubbly liquid on her tongue; the salty tang of the sea mingling with her own jasmine perfume and Mike's scent of musk and spice; the silky breeze caressing her skin.

She touched her lips to a throbbing cord of Mike's throat. "I'll never forget this night," she said huskily. "No matter what happens, I'll remember it for always."

Losing track of which of them was being seduced, Mike felt his body hardening against Caitlin. "Then it's a night neither of us will ever forget," he murmured, dipping his head to bring his mouth close to hers.

She could feel and taste the kiss that was just a breath away. But he held back, teasing mercilessly with a promise. "I think I need some more champagne," she managed to say when she could bear the suspense no longer.

Mike raised his own glass to Caitlin's mouth, gently stroking the crystal rim over her lower lip.

A shaft of acute need shot through Caitlin, and champagne was the least of her desires, but she took a sip, then decided to play turnabout, offering Mike her glass. Trembling, she dribbled champagne on his chin. She stared at him for an instant, then impulsively leaned forward and lapped up the cool droplets with the tip of her tongue. Hunger suddenly exploded inside her; she heard Mike's muffled groan, and in the next instant was seeking his lips and tongue, exploring the hidden pleasures of his mouth and offering her own to his avid probing. Still carelessly holding her glass of champagne, she wrapped both arms around his neck and was crushed against him as he enfolded her.

Lost in pleasure, Mike thought vaguely that he would like to get rid of the wine goblets, but he wasn't willing to release Caitlin long enough to do it. He felt as if he would never be willing to release her, for any reason. She was liquid sweetness, luscious and warm and eager, her body fitting against his as if made to be molded to him.

But he accidentally tipped his glass just enough to splash part of its contents over the rim, sending a shiver through Caitlin as the cold champagne began trickling slowly down her spine.

More excited than startled by the sudden sharp contrast between the icy liquid and the heat from Mike's hands on her sensitive skin, Caitlin willingly cooperated as he untwined her arms from around his neck, took her glass to set it and his own on the tray, then put his hands on her shoulders to turn her around.

"Allow me," he said. He bent his head and caught the cold rivulet of wine on his tongue just as the crisp liquid approached the first dark slash of Caitlin's dress straps. With both hands resting on her waist, he brushed his lips upward along her spine, licking at the champagne, intoxicated by the taste of Caitlin. Reaching the nape of her neck, he didn't stop. He blazed a trail of kisses along one of her shoulders, exerting enough pressure on her waist to turn her again to face him, then went on grazing his lips over her skin, finally moving to capture her mouth.

Every shred of Caitlin's resistance had been destroyed, every inch of her body charged with erotic pulsations. The more demanding Mike's kisses became, the more she ached to give to him and take from him. She thrilled to his touch as he smoothed one hand down over her hip to the high slash of her skirt and began caressing her thigh. Vaguely, she heard the melodic phrases of "It Had to be You" in the background. *How perfect*, she thought as she gazed up at Mike, knowing her eyes were silently confessing her complete surrender as the singer crooned.

"Let's go some place more private," he said, his voice thick with desire as he gathered her into his arms.

Nuzzling into the warmth of his throat, Caitlin nodded. "Some place very private," she answered, then turned her face for one more kiss.

She was in a daze as Mike guided her back indoors, through the various lounges and down several sets of stairs, shunning the crowded elevators. She was standing in front of a cabin not far from her own before she fully realized where she was. "I knew you were a neighbor, but I had no idea you were so close to me all this time," she said quietly.

"I knew," Mike answered. "And I've been going crazy, thinking of you just a few staterooms away." As he unlocked his door, he tried to set aside the doubts that had begun nagging at him once the magic of dancing under the stars had been replaced by the noise and lights indoors. Caitlin wanted him as much as he wanted her, he told himself as he hung the Do Not Disturb sign on his door.

But as he led her into the main room and stopped beside his spacious bed, he realized that he couldn't go through with a seduction that had begun as a ploy to gain control over her, to bend her to his will.

The reflection of the moon on the water was sending soft beams of light through the wide porthole of his darkened cabin, illuminating the trust in Caitlin's eyes. "I have to tell you something," he said with difficulty. "This whole evening—well, not the whole evening. Just since that drink we had before dinner. But since then, when I decided to make love to you, everything I've said and done has been part of a concerted effort to get you into my bed." He waited for her to explode and slam out the door.

"And?" she asked, tipping back her head to look up at him in obvious puzzlement. "Have I done something to change your mind?"

Mike scowled. "You don't understand, honey. It's all part of my tiresome need to be in control. I decided to have you, and here you are."

A tiny upward tilt appeared at the corners of her mouth. "You're adorable, you know that?"

The woman was going to drive him out of his mind, Mike decided. "I'm what?"

She kissed his chin, then brushed her lips along his tense jawline to his ear before whispering, "I may be scatterbrained, Mike Harris, but I'm not stupid. I know when I'm being seduced." Cradling his face between her palms, she gave him a mischievous grin. "Don't you?"

It took Mike several moments to absorb the implication of her words. "When?" he finally asked. "When did you make up your mind to turn the tables?"

"I didn't turn the tables," Caitlin said with sudden gravity. "I just reached the point when I knew it was foolish to keep battling my feelings for you." She smiled again and tugged on his bow tie to undo it. "As to when it happened, I'm not sure. It was some time between the appetizer course and the spilled champagne."

Carefully removing the studs from his shirt, Caitlin pretended not to notice that Mike was staring at her in shock. She'd told him the truth; she didn't know when or how or why she'd surrendered to the overpowering hunger to be close to him in every possible way, never mind the future or the fact that they weren't right for each other or that the courses of their lives were about to diverge. She simply knew that she would be diminished irreparably if she hid from the need to become part of him even for a little while. It was possible that she lied to herself about a lot of things; she couldn't lie to herself about her feelings for Mike. Not anymore.

She reached beyond him to put the gold studs on the top of the bureau, then returned her hands to his chest, sliding one palm under his shirt and over the hard, muscled expanse with its silky pelt. Her mouth sought his; she nibbled gently with her teeth and stroked with her tongue, coaxing a low groan from deep in his throat.

As if coming out of a trance, Mike cupped Caitlin's head in his two hands, his fingers laced through her hair as he responded to her teasing mouth with a deepening of his own explorations of its sweet, dark recesses.

Caitlin's hunger for Mike began intensifying. She tugged at his shirt. There was no shyness in her; she wanted him too much to be shy.

"Maybe I should help," he said with a low rasp, shrugging out of his jacket and tossing it aside, then methodically but shakily undoing his cufflinks and cummerbund, mentally cursing formal wear for being so difficult to remove.

"Maybe we both should help," Caitlin said, smiling, excited to see how deeply Mike was affected.

They undressed each other slowly, savoring each moment and touch and kiss. Mike traced the lines of Caitlin's dress straps to the tie that held them, then with a quick pull began the unlacing he'd ached to do all evening.

As his fingertips feathered over her back, loosening her dress with excruciating patience, Caitlin pushed his shirt off his shoulders. Mike paused in his efforts just long enough to lower his hands to his sides and let the shirt drop to the floor, and Caitlin thrilled to the sheer male power of the rippling muscles under his bronzed skin; she delighted in the contrast between the smoothness of his back and the hair-roughened texture of his forearms and chest.

She was almost faint with pleasure when her bodice finally slid down to her waist, and Mike cupped his hands over her breasts. Releasing her mouth at last, he looked down at her, his eyes like dark, smoky velvet. "Caitlin, you're so lovely," he murmured, gently kneading her soft flesh. "Since yesterday I haven't been able to stop thinking about how cool and hot you are at the same time, how you feel under my hands, how you respond. . . ." He felt her nipples swelling against his palm and watched her eyes glaze over with moisture as her need heightened.

"Help me again," she said with a touching urgency as she fumbled with the fastenings on his waistband.

Mike quickly rid himself of his remaining clothes, then pushed Caitlin's dress downward over her hips so that it slid the rest of the way to the floor. A moment later her black bikini panties joined the dress, and Caitlin was naked in Mike's arms, her feminine contours molding themselves to him, his hard maleness pulsating against her belly, his mouth once again claiming hers in a deep, probing kiss.

Caitlin herself was hardly aware of what she was doing when she smoothed her hands downward over his lean waist and along his hipbones, her fingers lightly stroking the crease of his thighs, tantalizing him by approaching yet never quite touching the center of his need. When at last she curled her fingers around him, Mike made a low, helpless groan.

Suddenly, he swept her up in his arms and carried her to the bed, stretching out beside her.

But Caitlin revealed a streak of unpredictability, coaxing him to his back and beginning an intense but leisurely tour of his body that pushed him to the limit again and again and again. Her hands explored, her lips teased, her tongue tasted. She caressed him even with her breasts; she pressed her cheek against his thigh and rubbed like a kitten.

Mike had never experienced anything like Caitlin's loving torment. He'd never known how sweet a surrender could be. He'd never trusted anyone that much.

Caitlin was amazed by her boldness and the aggressiveness of her desire. She didn't know what had made her take the reins from Mike, but she reveled in the sense of female power and freedom she was experiencing for the first time. By his consent Mike was hers to enjoy. And she was enjoying him to the fullest.

She straddled him, took him into her, rode him as if he belonged to her and existed only for her pleasure. Her head tipped back and her body arched as his hands roved continuously over her torso.

Sensing that she was nearing her peak and that his own explosion was imminent, Mike gripped Caitlin's hips tightly and thrust upward, no longer satisfied to be passive, driven by a primitive, irresistible instinct.

Feeling the change in him, Caitlin exulted in it. She was ready to surrender. Eager. When Mike suddenly tumbled her to her back and imprisoned her in his arms, she cried out and clung to him as he carried her to the ultimate summit.

A great wave of ecstasy welled up inside her, gathering strength and intensity until she thought she could bear no more, then burst like a river crashing through a dam. In the next instant she felt every muscle and sinew in Mike's body stiffen, hold, then let go, and it was as if the two of them clung to each other for dear life as the rushing waters swept them toward an unknown destination.

Finally, they reached a place where they were drifting, lulled by a gentle pool of bliss. But even as they rested quietly in each other's arms, both Caitlin and Mike were thoughtful and troubled.

Neither of them had been prepared to be so over-whelmed by what they'd shared. They'd shot the rapids successfully, but for the first time Caitlin understood what was meant by a river of no return.

And Mike knew a waterfall or two still waited ahead.

Ten

Caitlin padded barefoot about her cabin wearing a cotton kimono, trying not to think too much as she packed her suitcases and placed them in the corridor, to be taken away for holding and sorting before the next day's disembarkation. Mike was doing the same chore in his room before returning to spend the last night in her bed.

The last night, she mused with disbelief. Where had the evening gone? Where had the day gone?

As she folded a pair of slacks and placed them in the last bag she had to pack, Caitlin smiled ruefully. She knew exactly where the day had gone. It had sped by in a blur of shared passion as she and Mike had done their best to be sociable and friendly with the other passengers but had kept stealing back to his room or hers for another of their wild, greedy unions, as if they were trying to make up for lost time—past and future.

Nothing's over yet, she reminded herself as she packed her toiletries and makeup. Mike would be staying in London for a couple of days and so would she. Of course, he would be busy with his medical convention and would be staying at the elegant St. James Court, and she had decided to stick with her original plan to bunk in with Pam, so there would be no special intimacy of shipboard life to sustain the magic. But at least there wouldn't be a final good-bye as soon as the *QE2* docked in Southampton.

Caitlin sighed heavily, realizing that it wouldn't matter when she had to part from Mike once and for all: She'd have to face the separation sooner or later, and she'd learned the hard way that their closeness had made the unpleasant reality infinitely more difficult.

She wondered if she'd believed she could emerge more or less unscathed from an intense but brief affair with Mike. Now that she knew what it was to feel the warmth and strength of his arms, the joy of being filled by him, the contentment of falling asleep with his breath against her skin, and the thrill of waking up to his smile, how could she go on with the life she'd planned?

She stiffened her spine. When there was no choice, a person simply did what was necessary.

But was there a choice?

Caitlin gave her head a quick, violent little shake to clear it of that kind of nonsense. Even if she were naive enough to believe in something lasting with Mike, he hadn't made any such suggestion. Obviously, he knew their personalities and outlooks were too different. In real life they would drive each other around the bend in no time.

In any case, Caitlin told herself firmly, she was eager to get started on her trek, if only to get it out of her system. She would sit under a chestnut tree in the middle of a rolling green field, enjoying the peaceful solitude. Aunt Penny had loved Britain and missed being able to visit it, so Caitlin planned to write volumes about the people, the cottages and gardens, the tastes and smells of Cornish pasties and strong English ale in smoky village pubs.

And there was Oxford to look forward to: the park where her parents had met the year Caitlin's mother had visited the ancient university town; the footbridge in the public gardens when John Grant had proposed to Maureen Sullivan and had decided on the spot to move to her home state of Wisconsin and build a whole new life there; the gargoyles that had inspired a series of snapshots that had made Caitlin laugh uproariously when she'd been little, amazed that her parents had ever been young and silly enough to make such grotesque faces into a camera.

Sighing, Caitlin picked up her bag and took it out to the corridor just in time to see Mike striding toward her, carrying just his briefcase and wearing the taupe linen suit he'd had on when she'd seen him for the first time. Her pulse began racing and a bubble of bittersweet happiness welled up inside her as she let him into the cabin.

"My tie's in my pocket, and my briefcase is big enough to hold my other essentials," he explained, putting down the case and drawing Caitlin into his arms. "The rest of my luggage has been picked up already."

"Where's your robe?" she said teasingly. "Your nightshirt?"

Mike chuckled quietly and began moving his hands over her body in a way that had become familiar to her, a signal of delights to follow. "I guess I forgot them," he murmured just before his mouth claimed hers.

They made love all night with passionate desperation, pausing only for short naps, then waking to love again.

Morning was upon them before Caitlin was ready to face it. She burrowed against Mike as if she could hide for just a little longer, and he held her as if he felt the same way.

"Caitlin," he said as he absently stroked the curve of her hip and thigh. "There's something I want to say to you. One suggestion I'd like you to think about. No discussions at this point. Just think about it for a while, and we can talk later."

Caitlin raised her head from its resting place on his chest and smiled quizzically at him. Was he going to give her the lecture he'd been suppressing so successfully, the one she'd been braced for, the stern advice about joining up with a guided tour for her Cotswolds hike? He'd been remarkably quiet on that subject, considering his initial reaction. But how could she mind if he did launch into a speech about how foolish she was? Would she prefer he didn't care? "Okay, Doc, shoot," she said, returning to the nestling position she'd been enjoying so much.

He took a deep breath, then let it out slowly. "You know I'm scheduled to fly back to New York next Tuesday."

Caitlin knew only too well. After the convention Mike's time was going to be taken up with tours of various British clinics, and then he would be on his way home, back to his normal, well-planned, perfect life. End of story, she thought, steeling herself against the terrible sense of loss that pervaded her whole being.

Mike took another breath, then once again exhaled as if on a controlled count. "Go with me," he said at last.

Caitlin was perfectly still for several moments. "What are you suggesting?"

"Just what I said. Go back to New York with

me next Tuesday. I think we need time, Caitlin. We need to get to know each other."

"Have you forgotten that we're not suited to each other at all?" she asked carefully.

"And have you forgotten that I asked you just to think about my suggestion?" Mike shot back. "No discussion, remember? You agreed, and I'm holding you to it."

Caitlin sat up, thrilled—and suddenly terrified. "You drop that one on me and say we're not going to discuss it?"

"I said we should talk later. Give the idea a chance to germinate."

And take root, Caitlin thought as her heart began pounding violently. And anchor one Caitlin Grant to the ground until one Mike Harris had his fill of her. And then a loneliness she wouldn't be able to bear. She swung her legs over the side of the bed and stood up. "What would be the point of my going back with you?" she said carefully, raking the fingers of both hands through her hair. "A trial . . . trial . . . trial *courtship* or something? We already know how it would end."

Mike watched her with deep satisfaction. Her reaction was everything he'd hoped for. And she was glorious, he thought as his gaze moved slowly and appreciatively over her lithe body. "No discussion," he said stubbornly.

"Oh, right," Caitlin muttered, grabbing her kimono and pulling it on. "A discussion isn't on the schedule, and we must stick to the damned schedule at all costs."

"You're scared," Mike said calmly. "All I want is for you to get over your initial panic so we can talk sanely about the possibility."

"Panic? *Panic?* I am *not* panicking!"

Clasping his palms behind his head, Mike smiled. "My mistake. I'd have sworn you were.

The shaky voice, the flush creeping over your breasts and throat, the stark terror in your eyes . . . But symptoms can be misleading. Maybe what you are is excited. Maybe you like the idea of staying with me. Maybe you're no more sure than I am that it would end badly. And maybe that's what scares you most of all. Most creatures tend to stick with the familiar, you know, even if it's not the greatest. I think you're so used to loneliness, you're not sure you could adjust to being without it. So you arrange your life to make sure you're good and lonely—except for your continuing devotion to Aunt Penny. Who, by the way, presents another difficulty. Out of gratitude and guilt and honest affection you've made a big emotional investment in your aunt, Caitlin. So you have to be wondering what she'd think of me, whether she'd say you're copping out by giving up your independent plans to take a chance on me. On us."

Caitlin glared at him. "This is your idea of not discussing something?"

"Sorry," Mike said with a grin. "I got carried away."

A muscle worked in her jaw as Caitlin tried to think of some comeback to everything Mike had said. "I'm going to have my shower now," she finally snapped.

"Would you like company?" he called as she marched into the washroom.

Caitlin's cheeks flamed as she remembered the last shower she'd had—with Mike for company. No wonder he thought she would go anywhere he asked, like some camp follower. She'd spent the past thirty-odd hours *doing* anything he asked, and coming up with a few shameless variations of her own!

She slammed the bathroom door and locked it.

As the sound of Mike's laughter infuriated her further, she turned on the shower full blast to drown him out.

She only hoped she could drown out the sudden shouting of her own inner voices as they heaped doubt and confusion on her without mercy.

Mike's laughter faded as soon as he knew Caitlin couldn't hear him; he let out a sigh of relief.

He'd been worried that he'd read Caitlin all wrong, that she would react differently. If she'd been calm and reasonable about refusing to go back to New York with him, even if she'd serenely accepted his temporary embargo on discussing the matter, he'd have known her feelings for him weren't very profound. He'd have known the same thing if she had accepted his vague invitation too readily—though he'd have been willing to build on the foundation of her eagerness.

But her sudden eruption and flight had told him what he'd wanted to know: Caitlin cared more for him than she wanted to. Than she dared to. His suggestion had shaken her very badly.

All he had to do was overcome every last one of the obstacles she was at this very moment thinking up. And then . . .

"Oh no!" he suddenly heard from the bathroom.

He was out of bed instantly. "What's wrong!" he shouted. "Caitlin, are you all right?"

He heard the shower being turned off, then Caitlin uttering a stream of salty curses he hadn't imagined she knew.

"Honey, what's going on in there?" he demanded, then tried the door. "Good Lord, did you scald yourself, Caitlin?"

Suddenly, the door opened and she stood staring at him, water streaming from her hair over her nude body and into a puddle around her feet. "My shampoo! It's gone!"

Mike blinked. "Shampoo?" he repeated, suddenly furious with her for giving him such a scare over nothing. "You're making this kind of fuss about *shampoo*? For crying out loud, use mine. I'll get it out of my briefcase."

"You don't understand," she cried. "I just remembered putting my shampoo in my overnight bag!"

Mike nodded, willing her to make sense. "Okay, so we'll get it from your overnight bag. Where is it?"

Caitlin slowly wagged her head from side to side. "I put it out in the corridor last night. Would you . . . would you look outside to see if it's still there?"

Mike grabbed two towels, wrapping one around Caitlin and the other around his own waist, surprised that she would make so much of such a small problem.

He opened the cabin door enough to glance out into the hall, then closed it and returned to Caitlin. "It's gone."

"Is there any way to get it back?"

"Not according to my cabin steward," Mike answered, frowning. "Once the bags have been taken, there's no retrieving them until we disembark." An awful thought began forming in his mind. "Caitlin, are you saying . . . surely you didn't . . . Honey? Did you . . . ?"

Caitlin nodded. "Every stitch," she said, her eyes enormous. "Even my shoes. I was so concerned with remembering to pack everything and trying to fit it in and separate what I'm leaving with Pam from what I'll want to take with me when I start hiking. I forgot to keep out what I needed for this morning. Mike, apart from my kimono . . ." She shook her head in utter disbelief. "Dear heaven, I never thought I'd say this and really mean it, but I haven't a thing to wear!"

Mike stared at her for several moments, then started chuckling. The chuckle gathered force until it was a rumble of laughter and he was clasping Caitlin against him.

"I'm glad you think it's so funny," Caitlin grumbled against his shoulder, though she was beginning to see the humor herself. Of all the times to be absentminded, why had she chosen her last morning with Mike?

"Honey, I'll just have a quick shower, get dressed, and go to one of the shops to buy something for you," Mike said cheerfully. "I've seen track suits in the sportswear place, and even some canvas shoes; they'll do until we get off the ship and pick up your suitcases, okay?"

Caitlin heaved a deep sigh, wondering what on earth she'd have done if Mike hadn't been around to get her out of this pickle.

"Honey, how do you expect me to watch you wander off by yourself in a strange country when you do things like this?" he said, still laughing out of sheer affection.

Caitlin stiffened. "Is that why you want me to go back to New York with you? Because you think I'm such an idiot I can't manage on my own?"

Mike winced, his laughter fading. What a time to make such a tactical error. "No, that's not why I want you to go back to New York with me. I've already told you why," he answered quietly. "But I have to admit, you make me want to take care of you, Caitlin. You bring out a protective urge in me. I can't help it."

Caitlin couldn't deny liking that particular tendency in Mike, but it wasn't enough. Suddenly, she realized that only one thing would be enough.

One brief but vital statement. And Mike hadn't made it.

Ridiculous, she told herself. How could she dare to hope for the words she had to hear before she changed her plans? She was being a childish romantic. She was being unfair. She was being a fool.

And yet she wanted him to say the words now, mean them now. *I love you, Caitlin. I can't let you go.* Even if Mike had to make a retraction later, she needed him to believe at this moment that he did love her. Because she loved him. It didn't matter that he represented everything she'd avoided for years and probably couldn't handle now: Order, permanence, practicality. She simply loved him, and it wasn't a shipboard infatuation that would end on dry land. "I guess you should have your shower before I go back and finish mine, or we'll run out of time," she murmured.

"Good idea," Mike answered, absently pressing a kiss to her forehead and releasing her.

He knew he'd lost a lot of ground with his careless teasing. He wondered if there was a way he could regain it. Unfortunately, for all his newfound insight into what made Caitlin tick, he still felt like a bumbling male when it came to fathoming her fascinating but maddeningly female mind.

When Mike found that the shops had closed for the ship's brief stay in port, he visited the purser. "I know it seems hard to believe a person could be so forgetful, Colin," he said after he'd explained what had happened, "but Miss Grant had a lot on her mind."

"It's not at all hard to believe," Colin Miller said good-naturedly, looking and sounding like some-

one right off the set of *Brideshead Revisited.*
"This sort of thing is more common than you
might expect. Unfortunately, Miss Grant's bag is
one of hundreds—thousands, in fact—in the luggage room. Perhaps if she asked a cabin stewardess—they often manage to come up with some
rudimentary bit of clothing to tide one over until
disembarkation."

"The stewardess did offer, but Caitlin's too tall,"
Mike pointed out. "If this sort of thing is common, there must be something that can be done,"
he said pleasantly but insistently. "Especially for
a passenger who pitched in to help your people
the way Caitlin did when she modeled in the fashion show on the second day of the voyage."

A light seemed to go on in the purser's head.
"Oh, *that* Miss Grant. Of course! I should have
recognized the name. It's unusual enough—the
Caitlin part, I mean. Even before she did us the
favor of taking part in the fashion show, we
were instructed to take good care of her. It seems
that someone, perhaps a clipping service, sent
our public-relations office a delightful newspaper
column Miss Grant had written, all about how
she'd always dreamed of a voyage on the *QE2* and
was about to see that dream come true. Evidently,
she promised a follow-up about whether the
crossing was everything she'd hoped. Good heavens, we shall have to do *something* for the lady.
Let me make a phone call or two; perhaps I can
find one of the shop people."

A phone call or two, Mike thought as he waited,
realizing that he hadn't given a single thought to
trying to reach the clinic since the day before last,
hadn't experienced a moment of dead-zone frustration since he'd set his mind on Caitlin. Amazing. Obviously, his priorities had undergone a
major shift.

Within half an hour Mike was back at Caitlin's cabin, carrying a plastic bag from the sportswear shop.

She made him feel like a conquering hero. He liked the sensation.

As he sat in the armchair where he'd first made love to her—and it had been lovemaking in the best sense, he now realized, despite the scruples that had made him stop—Mike watched with pleasure while Caitlin modeled the green-and-white track suit and white espadrilles he'd bought.

"You can take the credit for this one yourself," he said modestly, then explained what the purser had told him.

Caitlin was surprised. "That silly little column from a neighborhood weekly? I've heard of the power of the press, but this is ridiculous." She thought about it for a moment, then laughed. "Aunt Penny must have sent the column to the Cunard office. It's just the sort of thing she'd do. But imagine getting an upgrade out of it." She grinned and decided to make a confession. "I'll admit something to you. I've been curious all along, but I was afraid if I asked, somebody would realize there was a mistake and I'd be shipped back to my proper category, and then there'd be no more intimate little dinners with a certain sexy doctor."

Mike wished they had time to make love again. When Caitlin uttered that kind of remark and looked at him the way she was looking at him now, his whole being caught fire. He made up his mind then and there that he would do whatever it took to lure her back to the States with him. "If you're all set, let's go up to our table in the Queen's Grill for the last time and enjoy a huge breakfast," he said cheerfully. "Lord knows we need the calories for energy."

Caitlin laughed despite the pangs of sadness Mike's words gave her. The last time, she thought. Things were coming to an end too quickly. Wasn't there a way to make them slow down?

She stiffened her resolve. Caitlin Grant was a big girl, she told herself. She'd enjoyed a shipboard romance, and now the voyage was ending. No self-pity allowed. "By the way," she said lightly, taking her purse from a bureau drawer, "how much do I owe you for the outfit?"

Mike eyed the handbag with a rush of irritation. Did the woman have to be so independent? "More than you've got in cash or traveler's checks," he answered, reaching out to curl his hands around Caitlin's wrist and pull her onto his lap.

She paled. "Good Lord, did this outfit come from one of the designer's boutiques?" She didn't think so, but she'd been in such a fog all week. . . .

"Never mind about the outfit," Mike cut in. "What you owe me has nothing to do with money. You've turned my existence upside down, Caitlin Grant. You've made a shambles of my five-year plan. You've wrecked my sleep, made me more tired than when I started this supposedly restful voyage, forced me to question my whole way of life, totally destroyed my peace of mind. What you owe me now is a bargain."

Caitlin frowned, worried despite the thrills of excitement vibrating through her. "What kind of bargain?"

Mike hadn't gotten the details worked out in his own mind yet. And he had to call the clinic before he could confirm his part in the plan he was hatching. "I'll explain it to you later," he said. Then he cupped his hand behind Caitlin's head and pulled her down for a long, hard, possessive kiss that kept her too busy to argue.

Eleven

What seemed like a whole convoy of tugboats converged on the *QE2* as she approached the Port of Southampton. Caitlin and Mike leaned on the quarterdeck railing and watched in utter fascination as the small vessels manipulated the giant ship through a 180-degree turn, then pushed and pulled in a series of maneuvers that guided her through a narrow space right into her berth.

"It's like puppies rounding up an elephant," Caitlin remarked with a laugh, then was shocked to hear herself adding with total irrelevance to the conversation at hand, "I couldn't afford to live in New York."

Mike suppressed a smile. "You could stay with me for a while, couldn't you?"

Caitlin stared at him. "You've known me for five days and you're inviting me to live with you?"

"To *stay* with me," Mike said. "There's a difference." Even as he spoke, he realized he'd been rash when he'd issued that invitation. And being rash was yet another departure from his usual self. Where would it end? Why hadn't he stopped to think that Caitlin wouldn't allow herself to be that dependent on him? Since he'd started the ball rolling, however, he went with it. "Would it be so terrible to be my houseguest? Anyway, who says you couldn't afford it? You could build a terrific business in no time with your particular interest and skills."

Caitlin frowned. "What particular interest and skills?"

"Your ability to help older women look good and feel great about themselves. There wouldn't be anything wrong with offering classes or private consultations and charging a fee. You even have the talent to write a newsletter that would help build client loyalty. If you feel guilty about making too much money, I could steer you to a few places where you could salve your conscience with volunteer work. But to start with you could get referrals from our clinic as well as from some plastic surgeons I know. Health and a good self-image go hand in hand, Caitlin. You'd be performing an important service."

"And I'd be buying into the whole strive-for-success concept," Caitlin remarked automatically, though she couldn't help being intrigued by Mike's idea. Perhaps her beauty skills weren't just frivolous and useless. Perhaps Mike was right, and she *could* do something that mattered.

"I don't strive for success itself," Mike pointed out. "Not really. I do what matters to me, and the success follows. Isn't it time you stopped working so hard to be an underachiever when there's a crying need and a huge market for something you love to do?" He paused, then took a chance on saying the rest of what he had on his mind. "Isn't it time you quit leading the adventurous existence Aunt Penny can't have anymore and started on your own life?"

Caitlin said nothing for several long moments.

Finally, Mike had to break the silence. "Honey, if I'm out of line, say so. But I don't think I am."

Caitlin knew he wasn't. Yet she couldn't just let go of everything that she'd told herself for years mattered to her. "How long would this idyll last?" she asked. "What if I liked being your houseguest, and you felt like kicking me out after a couple of days?"

Relieved that she was giving his suggestion honest consideration, Mike burst out laughing and shook his head. There was one thing about Caitlin: She wouldn't let him get away with too much impulsiveness. Her essential integrity acted as natural brakes on both of them. "If I reached that point, I'd get one of the clinic psychiatrists to have a look at me. Give you up after a couple of days? Not a chance. Not after a couple of weeks, or months, or . . ." He stopped abruptly, just before he added the word *lifetimes.* Maybe he *should* go to talk to one of the clinic psychiatrists, he thought.

On the other hand, perhaps he was totally sane for the first time in his life. Perhaps he was discovering that buried deep within himself there was a core of confidence in the future and in his own judgment. Perhaps he didn't need his five-year plans anymore. "Look, I know it must seem strange to you that I, of all people, would do something so . . . so precipitate . . . as to ask a woman I barely know to ditch everything and just come home with me. I'm having trouble believing it myself. But on closer inspection I'm not sure I'm being as out of character as I seem."

"Sure you are," Caitlin said, not ready to hear him out even though she ached to believe him. "You're still under the spell of the ship. That's why you're being so . . ."—she smiled—"so *precipitate.*"

"I'm still under a spell, but the *QE2* isn't the sorceress," Mike shot back, ignoring Caitlin's gentle teasing. He reached up to cradle her face between his palms and spoke softly. "All right, honey, I mentioned a bargain a little while ago. The one I insist you owe me. Here's your part of it: You stay with me this week in London instead of going to your friend's place."

"We've talked about that," Caitlin said, steeling herself against giving in. "You'll be busy with your convention—you've admitted as much."

Mike grinned. "Okay, it's true that I'll be busy. But at least we could be together when I can sneak away. We can sleep in the same bed. We can make love. . . ."

"And tire you out even more?" Caitlin couldn't resist saying even as she felt her surrender beginning. Pitting her will against Mike's seemed to be a losing proposition. Or perhaps a winning one. She wasn't sure which.

Mike touched his lips to hers, a caress of aching sensitivity and tenderness. "Exhaust me," he murmured. "Exhaust both of us. What's wrong, Caitlin?" he added with deliberate challenge. "Aren't you up to one of life's *real* adventures?"

Caitlin slumped against him. "You're rotten, Mike Harris. Totally, unapologetically, terminally rotten."

Mike smiled as he wrapped his arms around her. "That means you'll stay with me for the week, right?"

Standing outside a fish-and-chips place in London's theater district, Caitlin waved as she saw Pamela Jennings rushing toward her, looking uncharacteristically businesslike in a white pleated skirt and navy linen blazer.

"Isn't it a perfect day we've ordered up for you?" Pam said as she threw her arms around Caitlin and hugged her. "You found the place without any trouble?"

"It was a piece of cake," Caitlin answered, laughing with pure pleasure. Pam was blond, blue-eyed, absolutely breathtaking, and living proof that the legendary English-girl complexion was no myth. She was also the one person her own age Caitlin had ever felt really close to. "You knew enough to skip the north-here-west-there directions and give me instructions in language that means something to me."

"Wonderful!" Pam said as she led the way into the small restaurant. "I'm proud of you. You honestly didn't get lost once?"

"I didn't say that," Caitlin admitted with a laugh. "I got lost in the Liberty Department store and went out the wrong door, but all I had to do was ask a bobby to point the way to the Palladium, and I had the whole thing aced."

"Save us a table," Pam said. "I'll go to the counter to get the goodies."

Caitlin found an empty spot and sank into a chair, relieved to rest after her nonstop morning—after two nonstop days, in fact. Even in comfortable flats and cool cotton slacks, she was feeling the effects of trying to cover all London's museums, endlessly fascinating shopping areas, and glorious parks in record time. She'd been filling her days with enough activity to crowd out troubled thoughts.

"I'm so sorry I've been tied up all week," Pam said as she returned with a tray of golden fish fillets and chunky fries doused with malt vinegar. "Imagine, here you are in London, and it's taken us ages to get together. And now, pet, just what is my favorite Yank up to these days?"

"Let's catch up on you first," Caitlin said, not ready yet to talk about Mike and the confusing choices she was faced with.

Pam willingly explained her new job in the public-affairs branch of a bank, spoke with sardonic humor about the current state of her love life— "in hiatus," she called it with an eloquent roll of her eyes—and spoke longingly of Los Angeles smog. But inevitably she turned the tables. "Now back to you. What about this lap of luxury you're living in, sailing first class on the *QE2* and staying at places like the St. James?"

"I'm not sure," Caitlin answered sincerely. "I think I'm out of my depth. Do people really live this way on a regular basis?"

Pam grinned as she lifted her slender shoulders in a shrug much like one of Caitlin's. "How should I know, pet? *I* certainly don't. But I trust you're not complaining. I assure you, a large, male-occupied bed at the St. James is more comfortable and certainly more rewarding than a single and empty cot in my flat."

"Oh, I'm not complaining at all. It's been wonderful. But . . ." Caitlin sighed. "The truth is, I've fallen hopelessly in love with an impossible man."

Pam's forehead creased in a worried frown. "Oh, you poor baby. And you've always been so cautious! But listen, it happens. Practically everybody trips over a married man at some point. The thing to do is drop him immediately. That cot at my flat isn't so uncomfortable, really."

Caitlin shook her head. "No, it's nothing like that. He's single."

"What, then? You did say he's a doctor, not a drug baron or an illegal arms dealer, did you not?"

"He's a doctor," Caitlin said with a laugh. "Just this morning he gave a lecture at an international medical convention." She looked at her watch. "It must be over. I tried to reach him just before you arrived, to find out how it went. But he still hadn't got back to the room."

"What *is* your problem?" Pam persisted. "Doesn't this perfectly single, internationally esteemed physician care for you in return?"

Caitlin sighed. "I'm not sure. Well, I know he cares for me. After all, he's asked me to go back to the States to stay with him. But he hasn't said he loves me."

"Good Lord, the cad! And you've known him a week!"

Caitlin smiled sweetly. "We don't need your British sense of irony here, Pamela."

"And we don't need your old dodging tricks here, Caitlin. You always were afraid someone would come along and sweep you off your feet. You were terrified you'd discard your silly vow to remain a spinster all your life. By the way, how's Aunt Penny?"

It was unsettling, Caitlin thought, the way Pam and Mike said the same kinds of things to her. "I didn't use the word *spinster*," she protested mildly. "I just said I thought marriage was overrated and outdated. And Aunt Penny's health could be better, but she's as feisty and cheerful as ever. That was a strange juxtaposition of thoughts."

"What was?"

"My vow to be a spinster and my aunt's health."

Pam chewed thoughtfully on a chip before saying any more. "You don't see the connection?"

"You mean because Aunt Penny never married?"

"Must I go over this ground again?" Pam said with exaggerated frustration. "All right: With very good reason, you admire your aunt enormously. But I remember when I used to listen to the stories about her exploits I sometimes thought you wished you could *be* Penelope Sullivan. I also believe you've spent years feeling guilty because she was called upon to settle down for a bit and take care of you."

Guilt, Caitlin thought, remembering Mike's almost identical words. She began pushing her food around on her plate, her appetite suddenly gone. "Aunt Penny never made me feel that way," she protested quietly.

"I didn't suggest she did. Merely that you jumped to that ridiculous conclusion. Children do that sort of thing, you know. But they have to outgrow it." Suddenly, Pam shook her head, swinging her long blond hair. "What a miserable stick I am, being so hard on you when we haven't seen each other in over a year. I'm just worried, luv. I want you to be happy, and it sounds as if you've stumbled onto a real man for a change. Tell me, what's he like?"

Although she knew Pam's heart was in the right place, Caitlin had endured enough. A real man for a change? She gave in to the temptation to submit her friend to a mild put-on. "Well, *I* find Michael attractive," she answered, then bit into a piece of generously battered fish and pretended to have to think hard to come up with just what was attractive about him. "He has a very nice personality, for one thing. He's gentle, easy to get along with, never gives me a moment's trouble. Really, Pam, he's such a darling little . . . lapdog! I do have to admit he would look better if he would get his nose reset, and I hope I can persuade him to stop combing those two cute little strands of hair from one ear to the other, as if they really cover his adorably shiny pate." She paused to enjoy Pam's suddenly bland, half-sick smile before returning her attention to her food and going on with more devilment than ever. "But you know, it's amazing how I've gotten over that silliness about wanting a man to be my height or taller. It's kind of cozy being able to rest my chin on the top of my sweetie's head when we dance." She glanced up in surprise when Pam didn't catch on and explode with amused outrage.

But Pam suddenly wasn't paying the least bit of attention. Her cornflower-blue gaze was fixed on the doorway. "I say, you may keep your darling doctor with the nice personality, pet. I'll take this one, thank you very much."

Caitlin turned and nearly fell off her chair. "Mike! What are you doing here?"

"Mike?" Pam repeated. "As in *your* Mike? Say it isn't so. Please. There has to be some justice in this world."

Mike gave the woman a vague smile, then beamed the full force of his crooked grin at Caitlin. "One of the speakers did a no-show, so I went on early and finished an hour ago. I'm a free man, honey. And I've been chasing all over the place trying to catch up with you. Those directions you wrote down were accurate but weird. Whatever happened to simplicity, like turn north on Regent, then east . . . ?" He stopped, realizing Caitlin's companion was giggling. "Sorry. I'm interrupting."

"Oh, interrupt away, darling," Pam said eagerly. "Care for some fish and chips?"

"Are they good here?" Mike asked.

"Simply marvelous," Pam assured him. "Self-serve, however."

Mike looked questioningly at Caitlin. "Really, I don't mean to intrude. I just didn't want to lose you for the whole afternoon to some obscure art gallery."

"You're not intruding at all," Caitlin said. "Pam's been asking about you; now she can get her information firsthand." But not too firsthand, she added silently as she introduced the two.

"Caitlin's been raving about how utterly, madly divine you are," Pam said, showing her dimple. "Even so, she's guilty of understatement."

Mike laughed self-consciously and went to the counter.

"There's no time for me to be diplomatic," Pam said the instant Mike was out of earshot, "so please understand that what I'm about to say is meant in the spirit of sincere and loving friendship. Grow up, Caitlin dear. If you let that simply super male get away from you because of heaven-knows-what fears and hang-ups left over from your childhood, you're a bloody little fool and someone ought to shake some sense into you. And now, with that speech behind me, what I ought to do is tell Mike every word you said just before he arrived." Ignoring Caitlin's stunned expression, Pam adopted an air of mock fury. "Your chin resting on the top of his little bald pate? Well, let me tell you, I wouldn't mind resting *my* chin on *that* lovely head. It conjures up the most delightful fantasies, actually. . . ."

"Hands off," Caitlin said, only half-teasing as she came out of her shock. "Chins off too. And no more dimples, understand?"

Pam sucked in her cheeks and crossed her eyes, but by the time Mike returned, she was on her best behavior.

Caitlin fell a little more deeply in love with Mike during lunch. Accustomed to watching her dates and male friends flirt outrageously with Pam even when they didn't mean to, she was warmed by Mike's apparent failure to realize that Pamela Jennings, though a loyal friend who wouldn't flirt back deliberately, was practically irresistible to the entire male gender. But Mike was friendly. Simply friendly. Nothing more.

A sudden memory came back to Caitlin. Mike had told her he wouldn't be any woman's property. But he wouldn't be a cheat. When he hooked up with somebody, he wouldn't play around with anyone else.

Caitlin wondered, Was he serious about hooking up with her? After just a week, could he possibly be serious about such a thing?

More to the point, could she?

"I really must dash," Pamela suddenly said, leaping to her feet. "Let's try to get together on the weekend, shall we? Give me a ring, or if you're in my neighborhood, just wander by and . . ." Her blue eyes danced as she looked straight at Mike, allowing herself one devilish little dimple. "And knock me up."

Caitlin pressed the heels of her hands into her eyes and shook her head in despair as her friend turned at the shop door and waved innocently before making her exit.

"I think it's an English expression," Mike said, hoping he hadn't caused any dissension between the two women. "Doesn't it just mean knock on her door?"

"Pam's an incurable tease," Caitlin said, laughing affectionately. "She lived in the States long enough to know better than to use that line to an American."

"You're not upset, I hope. She was just kidding."

"How could I be upset?" Caitlin said softly. "When I'm faced all of a sudden with a bonus afternoon with you, when you made such an effort to catch up with me—" She stopped and frowned. "Come to think of it, after I wrote down the directions for meeting Pam here, I tore the sheet of paper off the pad and brought it with me. How could you have followed them if you didn't have them?"

Mike grinned. "If I hadn't become a doctor, I'd have gone to detective school to become the next Sam Spade. It was the old pencil-shading trick. The imprint of what you'd written was on the notepad."

Caitlin stared at him for a very long moment. He'd gone to even more trouble to find her than she's realized. Perhaps she should play detective herself and look hard at the evidence Mike was offering as a clue to his feelings. Couldn't she reach a conclusion about how much he cared for her? Were the words really all that important when the deeds told her so much? "Maybe we should stroll over to the scene of the Sherlock Holmes novels," she said absently, realizing she'd been quiet for too long.

"What's really going on behind those green eyes of yours?" Mike asked as Caitlin's expression threatened his sense of public decency, drawing him right to the brink of sweeping her up in his arms, carrying her out to the nearest cab, and taking her back to the hotel to keep her there for the entire weekend. "Come to think of it," he said aloud, "that's not a bad idea."

"What's not a bad idea?" Caitlin asked, suddenly alert, aware of a delicious sense of danger emanating from Mike. "Aren't we going sightseeing?"

He got to his feet. "In a way," he said very quietly, holding out his hand to her.

Caitlin took it, and as jolts of sensual electricity sizzled through her, she somehow knew they weren't about to head for Baker Street. It was elementary.

* * *

The bathtub in the suite was big enough for two and deep enough to allow for a lot of bubbles. Lounging against Mike while he generously lathered her torso with her favorite soap from the Body Shop, Caitlin inhaled the scent of apricots and wiggled just a little so she could feel the tickle of his chest hairs on her back.

"I'd advise you to be still," he said in a low, teasing growl as he kneaded the slippery mounds of her breasts, rolling the nipples between his thumbs and forefingers.

Arching into his hands, Caitlin laughed softly and gave her hips a slow, deliberate swivel. "Will I suffer a fate worse than death now?" She caught her breath as Mike spread the fragrant lather over her body in circles that ventured further and further downward. "Again, that is?" she barely managed to whisper. "I had no idea you could be so . . ." He placed the soap in one of Caitlin's hands and began massaging her stomach, his long fingers reaching ever closer to the sensitive spot between her thighs that he'd come to know so well. "So incorrigible," she finished on a sigh.

"Nor did I," Mike murmured. "You seem to inspire me."

Shakily, Caitlin tried to lather his encircling arms, but very soon her movements were erratic and helpless, her breathing as uneven as her heartbeat. She felt the bar of soap slipping from her hand, heard a quiet plop as it dropped into the tub. On fire, she twisted and pressed herself against Mike's hand. As if pouring oil on a conflagration, he began lapping water over her in tortuously gentle waves, then scooped up handfuls of the bubbly liquid and poured it on her shoulders so that it streamed down her body in shivery rivulets.

Finally, when the sweet torment had become unbearable, Caitlin turned until she was half-lying over Mike, her breasts sensitive to the wet, coarse silk of his chest hair. She captured his mouth, her tongue moistening his lips, then slipping between them and dipping in and out in a playfully taunting evocation of what she wanted from him, what she knew he loved to give her.

But he took his time, somehow finding the soap and lathering her back, the rounded curves of her buttocks, the backs and insides of her thighs. Then he splashed and poured water over her again until every fiber of her body was vibrating with pleasure and she was moving against him, trying to draw him into her, lacing her hands through his hair as her kisses became hungrier and more urgent.

Just when she thought she might go wild with need, Mike slid his hands under her hips, lifted, and slowly brought her downward until she was filled with him.

She had no control, and didn't want any as he gripped her hips with both hands, holding her body exactly where he wanted it. His thrusts were deep and strong and thrilling; she imagined she could feel his male power pervading every part of her, permeating every cell, reaching even to her fingertips. She was part of him, he of her, and when they exploded as one, the essence of him seemed to pour through her, infusing her entire being with his love.

Caitlin knew at that moment that she would go with Mike wherever he asked, whenever he wished.

*　　*　　*

She was nestled against him in bed, her head on his shoulder and her legs entwined with his, when he almost startled her by speaking. "Here's the plan," he said quietly but firmly.

Caitlin giggled. "A five-year plan?" she teased.

"Hell, no," Mike pretended to grumble. "I gave up on those when I looked up and saw you on the New York pier, whether I knew it or not at the time. No, this one's just a two-week plan. Our bargain. If you'll recall, I never did mention what my part would be."

Bargains, Caitlin thought. As if bargains had anything to do with what she felt for this man. But she was curious. "What is it, then?" she asked, letting her fingers toy lazily in the coils of dark hair on his chest.

"If you have no objection, I'm going to do the Cotswolds walk with you. Just for a week, but I'm hoping by the end of that time to have overcome your objections to going back to the States with me."

Caitlin had been about to press a kiss to his shoulder when his words had stopped her in a freeze-frame. "Once and for all, I take back what I said. Never again will I accuse you of being predictable. Now, what did you just suggest?"

Mike smiled and calmly repeated himself.

"You don't have to go through all this for my sake," Caitlin protested, though she was deeply touched. She propped herself up on one elbow to smile down at him. "I appreciate the thought, but it isn't necessary."

"Yes, it is," Mike said, reaching up to trace his index finger along her jawline. "I want to prove to you and to myself that I can be flexible, that I can cope with circumstances that aren't antiseptic and comfortable—"

"I told you I was sorry I made that crack," Caitlin said, glowering at him.

"I'm not. I'm glad you made it. You were right. And the very fact that I've fallen for you tells me that there are sides to me I've been suppressing, sides you bring out. I want to explore more than the English countryside, Caitlin. I want to explore myself, and you, and us." He grinned. "Anyway, I still think you'd wander into a bog if I weren't along to keep you on the proper path."

Caitlin glared at him, pictured what he'd suggested, then burst out laughing. "You're probably right. But what about the clinic?"

"I've called Dave," Mike answered with a grin. "He's glad I'm finally giving in and taking a little bit of time off. Everything's running smoothly without me—even my most loyal patients are coping perfectly well with my substitute. It seems I'm not indispensible after all."

"You are to me," Caitlin said softly. "I love you, Mike."

He gazed at her for a timeless, breathless moment. "I love you too, Caitlin."

Caitlin blinked. "You do?"

"Of course I do. You think a man turns himself inside out for a woman he doesn't love?"

She sat up and knelt on the bed to glare furiously at him. "Why didn't you *tell* me? Do you have any idea how much I ached to hear you say those words? Are you going to turn out to be one of those lovers who thinks the words aren't necessary? Because they are, Mike Harris! They're absolutely essential!"

Mike reached up and pulled her down over him, laughing. "Listen, you. When I asked you to come and stay with me in New York, you acted as if I'd lost all my marbles. After all, you said, we'd known each other for only a week. I didn't dare tell you I was hopelessly, helplessly, uncontrollably in love with you!"

Caitlin's lips curved into a smile. "Uncontrollably?"

Mike paused, then heaved a dramatically heavy sigh. "Uncontrollably," he repeated. He had the feeling that the controllable portion of his life was over. And the good part had just begun. But he felt he had to assert himself one last time. "By the way," he said lightly, "there's a part of the plan that I forgot to mention."

"Mmm?" Caitlin said languidly, too blissful to think. "What part of the plan?"

"I have to meet Aunt Penny."

Caitlin made a face. She didn't look forward to telling her aunt she'd abandoned the life of an adventuress in favor of love. But she'd been doing a lot of thinking, and she knew Pam was right . . . and Mike was right. Caitlin Grant had to live her own life, not be a surrogate for someone else. And at some point the restlessness that had plagued her for years had disappeared. She'd discovered the truth of another of Pam's theories: All she had to do to find her own identity was look inside herself.

She smiled at Mike. "I'll admit Aunt Penny might be a little concerned at first about my getting tied down," she told him. "But if anyone can get to her, I imagine it's you."

He didn't respond, and he was silent for such a long time that Caitlin raised her head to see if he'd fallen asleep. He hadn't. He was staring at the ceiling. She could almost see the wheels turning in his mind. "What are you thinking so hard about?" she asked.

"A scheme for winning Aunt Penny over," he answered.

Caitlin laughed. "That's sweet, but with or

without her approval I'm sticking with you, so you don't have to—"

"Of course I do," Mike said, suddenly putting both arms around Caitlin and rolling until she was under him. "When I ask the lady for your hand, Caitlin Grant, I want her on my side."

Epilogue

"My Lord, but you're a pushy, bullying son of a
. . ."

"Be nice, Aunt Penny," Mike interrupted with a
grin as he patted the wrinkled hand that was
tucked under his arm. "You're sounding like your
great-niece again." He clucked his tongue. "The
profanity my women use is deplorable. What am
I going to do with you two?"

Penelope Sullivan chuckled, but quickly caught
herself and heaved a martyred sigh. "I suppose
there's no way out of this walk," she grumbled.
"You'll natter at me until it's over with." Relenting, she smiled up at Mike. "And I guess I have
to admit I'm feeling better for sticking to the regi-
men you've imposed on me. But why can't I rest
on my laurels? Why do you insist that I take even
a couple of extra steps each day? Walking on the
sand is no day at the beach, you know."

Mike tipped back his head and laughed, then
hugged the diminutive white-haired woman who
was less stooped and pain-racked than when he
and Caitlin had moved to St. Pete's Beach a few
months before. The town had been ripe for an

178

SRDP clinic, and Aunt Penny had been willing to start fighting back against the ravages of her arthritis, with Mike's help. "No pun intended, of course," he teased.

Aunt Penny grinned, but fell silent as she concentrated on pushing her limits a little further. They had completed their walk and were back at their beach chairs when she suddenly stopped and shaded her eyes with one hand to watch a cabin cruiser cut through the waves far out on the water. "I'll never come to terms with being grounded," she said with a sigh. "There's so much world I never got to see."

"Let's put it this way," Mike pointed out, determined to keep his favorite patient in a positive frame of mind. "You thought you were confined to your house, or at least your little patio, and now you're going out every day for a stroll in the sun. Every one of the extra steps I nag you into taking is an unexpected bonus, right?"

Aunt Penny shook her head in mock despair. "Right," she conceded. "Are you this disgustingly optimistic and bossy with your wife?"

"Only when she needs it," Mike said cheerfully, then added fondly, "And she can be pretty tough on me when it's necessary. Don't underestimate Caitlin. Nobody pushes her around, including her husband."

"Where *is* the girl, anyway?" Aunt Penny said as she lowered herself into her chair. "I thought we were all going to have a picnic here at the beach."

"We are. She's probably spending extra time with her class at the community center," Mike fibbed, suppressing his own impatience. "Or maybe she's taken a wrong turn on the way. You know Caitlin."

Aunt Penny laughed affectionately. "Oh yes. I

know Caitlin." A moment later she added pensively, "I didn't always know her, though. Perhaps not until you came along. She always kept things to herself. Hid her feelings to the point where I gave up trying to guess what was really going on inside her. When did she start to open up? How did you manage it?"

"I don't know," Mike said as he sat cross-legged on the ground. "I think it was when we did our walking tour. We'd see a place she recognized from stories her folks had told her, and she'd tell me some little anecdote, often something she hadn't remembered until that very moment. There were a lot of tears shed, but there was laughter too. Caitlin's instincts were right when she planned that hike; it was like opening doors to long-locked rooms and letting in the light. All I did was listen, and hold her, and be there for her." Looking up, he suddenly saw Caitlin racing along the beach toward him in bare feet, her flat sandals hooked over two fingers, her coral dress hiked up to allow for her long strides, her short hair tousled by the breeze.

Mike took one look into her green eyes and knew.

She flew into his waiting arms. "You were right! I love you, Mike Harris! I'm crazy about you! I thought I'd never get here so I could tell you! You were absolutely right!"

Mike buried his face in the warmth of her neck, his happiness almost unbearable.

"One thing about you two," Aunt Penny pretended to grouse. "You're not shy about showing affection. What on earth is this insufferable young man right about now?"

Caitlin nestled against Mike's chest and smiled at her aunt. "It's awful being married to a doctor, Aunt Penny. Just awful."

"No doubt. But why do you admit it at this point?"

Looking up at Mike with shining eyes, Caitlin said, "Because he knew before I did. I've just come from having his diagnosis confirmed."

"Knew what?" Aunt Penny said with a note of alarm. "What diagnosis? Have you been ill, Caitlin?"

Caitlin laughed and hugged Mike again. "You tell her, wise guy."

Mike grinned. "My wife's going to be a mother, Aunt Penny. Just in time to beat her thirtieth birthday. Which will make you a great-great-aunt. What do you think about *that* kind of adventure?"

"Great-great-aunt?" she said in a small voice. "Dear, oh dear, how did I get to be so old?" After a sharp glance from Mike, Aunt Penny added hastily, "A great-great-aunt? Why, I can't think of anything more rejuvenating than having to keep up with a child spawned by you two. It's sure to be a first-class imp."

"He," Caitlin corrected her.

"She," Mike said.

They both laughed. "Whichever," Caitlin went on with a quiver of excitement in her voice, "we've got to start planning, thinking differently, considering the future, finding a place to live that's near parks and good schools, opening up a college savings account—"

"Caitlin," Mike cut in.

"Yes?"

He cradled her face between his palms and smiled. "Honey, there'll be lots of time for making those plans. For now, why don't we just enjoy?" He rubbed noses with her. "What you've got to learn, sweetheart, is to go with the flow . . . let life happen . . . forget about stage-managing."

The last thing Caitlin saw from the corner of her eye before she gave herself to Mike's sweet, loving, possessive kiss, was Aunt Penny's delighted, satisfied grin.

THE EDITOR'S CORNER

It's a pleasure to return to the Editor's Corner while Susann Brailey is away on maternity leave, the proud mother of her first child—a beautiful, big, healthy daughter. It is truly holiday season here with this wonderful addition to our extended "family," and I'm delighted to share our feelings of blessings with you . . . in the form of wonderful books coming your way next month.

First, let me announce that what so many of you have written to me asking for will be in your stockings in just thirty days! Four classic LOVESWEPT romances from the spellbinding pen of Iris Johansen will go on sale in what we are calling the **JOHANSEN JUBILEE** reissues. These much-requested titles take you back to the very beginning of Iris's fabulous writing career with the first four romances she wrote, and they are **STORMY VOWS, TEMPEST AT SEA, THE RELUCTANT LARK,** and **BRONZED HAWK**. In these very first love stories published in the fall and winter of 1983, Iris began the tradition of continuing characters that has come to be commonplace in romance publishing. She is a true innovator, a great talent, and I'm sure you'll want to buy all these signed editions, if not for yourself, then for someone you care about. Could there be a better Christmas present than an introduction to the love stories of Iris Johansen? And look for great news inside each of the JOHANSEN JUBILEE editions about her captivating work coming in February, **THE WIND DANCER**. Bantam, too, has a glorious surprise that we will announce next month.

Give a big shout "hooray" now because Barbara Bowell is back! And back with a romance you've requested—**THE LAST BRADY,** LOVESWEPT

(continued)

#444. Delightful Colleen Brady gets her own romance with an irresistibly virile heartbreaker, Jack Blackledge. He's hard to handle—to put it mildly—and she's utterly inexperienced, so when he needs her to persuade his mother he's involved with a nice girl for a change, the sparks really fly. As always, Barbara Boswell gives you a sweet, charged, absolutely unforgettable love story.

A hurricane hits in the opening pages of Charlotte Hughes's **LOUISIANA LOVIN'**, LOVESWEPT #445, and its force spins Gator Landry and Michelle Thurston into a breathlessly passionate love story. They'd been apart for years, but how could Michelle forget the wild Cajun boy who'd awakened her with sizzling kisses when she was a teenager? And what was she to do with him now, when they were trapped together on Lizard Bayou during the tempest? Fire and frenzy and storm weld them together, but insecurity and pain threaten to tear them apart. A marvelous LOVESWEPT from a very gifted author!

SWEET MISCHIEF, LOVESWEPT #446, by Doris Parmett is a sheer delight. Full of fun, fast-paced, and taut with sexual tension, **SWEET MISCHIEF** tells the love story of sassy Katie Reynolds and irresistible Bill Logan. Bill is disillusioned about the institution of marriage and comes home to his childhood friend Katie with an outrageous proposition. . . . But Katie has loved him long enough and hard enough to dare anything, break any rules to get him for keeps. Ecstasy and deep emotion throw Bill for a loop . . . and Katie is swinging the lasso. **SWEET MISCHIEF** makes for grand reading, indeed. A real keeper.

Bewitching is the first word that comes to mind to
(continued)

describe Linda Cajio's LOVESWEPT #447, **NIGHTS IN WHITE SATIN**. When Jill Daneforth arrives in England determined to get revenge for the theft of her mother's legacy, she is totally unprepared for Rick Kitteridge, an aristocrat and a devil of temptation. He pursues her with fierce passion—but an underlying fear that she can never be wholly his, never share more than his wild and wonderful embraces. How this tempestuous pair reconciles their differences provides some of the most exciting reading ever!

Witty and wonderful, **SQUEEZE PLAY,** LOVESWEPT #448, from beloved Lori Copeland provides chuckles and warmth galore. As spontaneous as she is beautiful, Carly Winters has to struggle to manage her attraction to Dex Mathews, the brilliant and gorgeous ex-fiance who has returned to town to plague her in every way . . . including competing in the company softball game. They'd broken up before because of her insecurity over their differences in everything except passion. Now he's back kissing her until she melts, vowing he loves her as she is . . . and giving you unbeatable romance reading.

Sweeping you into a whirlwind of sensual romance, **LORD OF LIGHTNING,** LOVESWEPT #449, is from the extraordinary writer, Suzanne Forster. Lise Anderson takes one look at Stephen Gage and knows she has encountered the flesh-and-blood embodiment of her fantasy lover. As attracted to her as she is to him, Stephen somehow knows that Lise yearns to surrender to thrilling seduction, to abandon all restraint. And he knows, too, that he is just the man to make her dreams come true. But her fears collide with his . . . even as they show

(continued)

each other the way to heaven . . . and only a powerful love can overcome the schism between this
fiercely independent schoolteacher and mysterious
geologist. **LORD OF LIGHTNING**—as thrilling a romance as you'll ever hope to read.

Six great romances next month . . . four great Iris
Johansen classics—LOVESWEPT hopes to make
your holiday very special and very specially romantic.

With every good wish for a holiday filled with the
best things in life—the love of family and friends.

Sincerely,

Carolyn Nichols

Carolyn Nichols,
Publisher,
LOVESWEPT
Bantam Books
666 Fifth Avenue
New York, NY 10103

P.S. GIVE YOURSELF A SPECIAL PRESENT:
CALL OUR LOVESWEPT LINE 1-900-896-2505
TO HEAR EXCITING NEWS FROM ONE OF
YOUR FAVORITE AUTHORS AND TO EN-
TER OUR SWEEPSTAKES TO WIN A FABU-
LOUS TRIP FOR TWO TO PARIS!

FOREVER LOVESWEPT

SPECIAL KEEPSAKE EDITION OFFER

$12⁹⁵

VALUE

Here's your chance to receive a special hardcover Loveswept "Keepsake Edition" to keep close to your heart forever. Collect hearts (shown on next page) found in the back of Loveswepts #426-#449 (on sale from September 1990 through December 1990). Once you have collected a total of 15 hearts, fill out the coupon and selection form on the next page (no photocopies or hand drawn facsimiles will be accepted) and mail to: Loveswept Keepsake, P.O. Box 9014, Bohemia, NY 11716.

FOREVER LOVESWEPT
SPECIAL <u>KEEPSAKE</u> EDITION OFFER
SELECTION FORM

Choose from these special Loveswepts by your favorite authors. Please write a 1 next to your first choice, a 2 next to your second choice. Loveswept will honor your preference as inventory allows.

$\heartsuit$ $\heartsuit$ $\heartsuit$ *Loveswept*®

_____BAD FOR EACH OTHER   Billie Green

_____NOTORIOUS   Iris Johansen

_____WILD CHILD   Suzanne Forster

_____A WHOLE NEW LIGHT   Sandra Brown

_____HOT TOUCH   Deborah Smith

_____ONCE UPON A TIME...GOLDEN
      THREADS   Kay Hooper

Attached are 15 hearts and the selection form which indicates my choices for my special hardcover Loveswept "Keepsake Edition." Please mail my book to:

NAME:_____

ADDRESS:_____

CITY/STATE:_____ZIP:_____

Offer open only to residents of the United States, Puerto Rico and Canada. Void where prohibited, taxed, or restricted. Allow 6 - 8 weeks after receipt of coupons for delivery. Offer expires January 15, 1991. You will receive your first choice as inventory allows; if that book is no longer available, you'll receive your second choice, etc.